Miracle Acupuncturist

28 Short Stories Based on the Unbelievable
Experiences of Dr. Liu's Patients

Miracle Acupuncturist

28 Short Stories Based on the Unbelievable
Experiences of Dr. Liu's Patients

HARRY J. HUANG

 Bestview Scholars Publishing

Published in 2022 by
Bestview Scholars Publishing Ltd.
48 Leafield Dr., Unit B., Toronto, ON M1W 2T2 Canada
Email: bestviewscholars@gmail.com
Website: **www.bestviewscholars.com**
Cover design: Alice W. Huang
The author thanks Paula Chiarcos for proofreading this book.
ISBN: 9-781896-848228
ISBN (epub) 9-781896-848235

Library and Archives Canada Cataloguing in Publication

Title: Miracle acupuncturist : 28 short stories based on the
  unbelievable experiences of Dr. Liu's patients / Harry J. Huang.
Names: Huang, Harry J., 1956- author.
Identifiers: Canadiana (print) 20220411220 | Canadiana (ebook)
  20220411247 | ISBN 9781896848228 (softcover) | ISBN
  9781896848235 (PDF)
Subjects: LCSH: Acupuncture—Fiction. | LCGFT: Short stories.
Classification: LCC PS8615.U211 M57 2022 | DDC C813/.6—dc23

This is a book of literary stories based on the positive experiences of world-renowned acupuncturist Dr. (PhD) Wan Cheng Liu's patients from different places in the world. The miraculous treatment results (claimed by patients and reporters) in this collection were all made available to the public in different languages by patients, news reporters, researchers, and other writers. They were either posted online or published in newspapers, magazines, books, or reported on TV in Budapest, Hong Kong, Regina, Markham, Toronto, or elsewhere. All the patients' names in this collection are fictitious. Due to unavailability of patient information prior to Dr. Liu's treatment, the author had to create, based on his imagination, this portion and other elements deemed necessary for a literary story. For this reason, all the stories and characters in this collection are to be considered fictional, and any resemblance of any person living or dead is to be considered coincidental. The publisher, author, and Dr. Liu are not responsible for any inaccurate description, if any, of any treatment methods and results. Neither do they recommend any type of medical treatment for patients. Ill persons should consult a conventional doctor before seeing an acupuncturist.

This is an original print edition of *Miracle Acupuncturist.*

To Dr. Wan Cheng Liu and all other role-model doctors of conventional medicine and alternative medicine.

Contents

A Single Needle for $100   1

A Real Doctor   8

Be a Real Woman Again   14

Secret Visits   18

"My Last Doctor"   25

Miraculous Height Increase   30

It's a Miracle   34

Problem with the Triplets   40

Life Regained   44

Miracle Acupuncturist   48

Bedtime Story for a 4-Month-Old   54

Birthday-ache   58

COVID-19 Patients   66

Alternative to Surgery   71

Encounter at a Party   77

Treating an Alzheimer's Patient   81

15 Years of Allergies Cured in 20 Days   86

Not a Doctor but a Deity   92

Speechless   96

Pride Put Aside   100

Is It Fate?   104

An Apology to Dr. Liu   108

Legs Nearly Lost   112

Mr. Shawl's Heart   116

Your Pulse Says It All   120

37 Years Vs. 30 Days   124

You Are Shortening My Life   137
About the Miracle Acupuncturist   142
Appendix   147

A Single Needle for $100

Last Monday, left-handed Lloyd Lorrial, a physician, was involved in a traffic accident outside his medical center at the intersection of two busy streets in East York. Lloyd knew he was injured albeit not severely. The ambulance took him to the hospital, but a comprehensive examination showed that he had no broken bones or other injuries, so he was discharged immediately.

As he remembered, the moment his car was swept onto the sidewalk, he lurched forward at least once. Right from the beginning, he suspected that something had happened to his upper body—it could be his sternum, arms, or neck. Everything happened so fast, and pinpointing the exact problem on his own body was not easy, though he was a physician himself.

When he woke up the next morning, he found his left arm hurting. At breakfast, he could still hold his plate, but in the afternoon, he could no longer write his prescriptions. Without hesitation, he canceled some of the patients' appointments and sought help from a neurologist in the same building.

At 4:30 p.m., Lloyd saw the neurologist, who examined him carefully and told him that his nerves were undamaged and that only the muscles of his left shoulder appeared to have been strained, which would take five days or so to recover. He prescribed no treatments and medications, only asking him to cover his injured shoulder with ice if it hurt badly, which Lloyd knew himself. Lloyd was disappointed that his visit had not improved his condition at all.

The following day, Lloyd saw a chiropractor, who was best

known for treating bone problems, especially shoulder pain. The chiropractor tried to realign Llyod's musculoskeletal system, but after three visits, Lloyd found the treatment ineffective. He was not even sure whether it had improved his condition or made it worse. He just felt that further treatment by the same chiropractor would be meaningless, and therefore, he gave up.

Though his injury was not as bad as a broken limb, the numbness and pain on the left arm just had to be cured one way or another, for he could not live or work without his left arm. When he returned to his own clinic after his third visit to the chiropractor on Friday morning, he thought of physiotherapy. But instead, he went upstairs in person to book an appointment with the best massage therapist on the top floor of the medical building. The massage therapist provided him with friction therapy on the same afternoon. He tried gently to break apart the adhesions that he suspected had been causing the pain and numbness, but Lloyd felt the pain was almost unbearable during the treatment. The massage therapist told him that he would feel better afterward. Lloyd endured another painful treatment the following day, but his condition deteriorated. On Monday, his left arm became stiffer, and he could not raise it anymore. It had become totally disabled.

How disappointed Lloyd was! He had the privilege of using the services of the medical professionals of the entire medical center, but who in the medical center, or the entire healthcare system, could cure his disabled arm? He hated to switch from one specialist to another, but he had no choice. Unwillingly, he canceled his third appointment with the massage therapist.

Isn't it ironic that a doctor who had access to the services of so many other doctors had become helpless? Lloyd grew more agitated and anxious, which also worried his wife, Karen.

"Lloyd," she said, "have you thought of trying acupuncture?"

"I have, but, honestly, I am always skeptical about the effect of acupuncture. That little needle alone. Nothing else at all. How could it possibly cure this big disabled arm? Oh, I don't know." He sighed as he patted his left arm.

"If you can find a good acupuncturist, you never know," said Karen. "Look, Lloyd, it has no side effects, because you don't need to take any medications. There is really no harm trying it once or twice to see if it works."

"You know what, Karen? Just three days before this damn traffic accident, I attended a conference on alternative medicine. There, I met a good acupuncturist, I think, a real one. He has a PhD in acupuncture. And he is in Toronto."

"How wonderful! Why not go and see him then?"

"Well," he said, shaking his head.

"Well? What?"

"Well, I did not show my due respect for him and his profession," he answered, looking guilty.

"What did you say and what did you do to him then?"

"Well," he said. "I didn't really say anything or do anything. He was presenting a study on acupuncture treatment for uterine fibroids. I just challenged him with several questions which he could not answer scientifically in front of a big audience. I just wanted to know how the needle worked, what happened when the needle was inserted into the patient's acupuncture point, or what specific changes really took place inside. I wanted some hard data. He had a PhD in acupuncture, and I thought he should be able to answer these questions. But he could not. He only used very vague ancient theory based on traditional Chinese medicine that just didn't make sense to me."

"Is that all?" Karen asked.

"Yeah, but I really feel ashamed of myself, for I think I may really have to go to see him," answered Lloyd.

"Well, since he has a PhD, he must be a scholar. And a scholar understands others' concerns. Maybe you were not the first or only person to ask him such questions. If he is a good acupuncturist, that's what matters. Lloyd, why not just apologize to him when you meet him?"

"You are right. Maybe I should really go for a try."

"Lloyd, you have tried every type of treatment available, and none worked for you. You need to give alternative medicine a chance. Do you have his phone number?"

"Nope. But I think I can easily find it online." With this he googled "Acupuncturist Wan Cheng Liu" and found his contact information immediately. "Karen, I've found it."

"Come on, I will drive you there right away," said Karen. "You can see him in person and then decide if you want to stay for his treatment. Ask your assistant to reschedule your appointments with your own patients. You will work way more efficiently when your arm is cured."

Lloyd called Dr. Liu and made an appointment with him. Half an hour later, he and Karen arrived at his clinic. Dr. Liu asked him to fill out a standard patient-information form, which he did. Then, he invited him to sit down and started to examine Lloyd's ailments. He felt his pulse using three fingers, applying different pressure on each. Then, he glanced at his face. During the diagnosis, he also talked with Lloyd.

"So, you are a doctor yourself in Toronto?" he said as he looked at Llyod's form.

Lloyd nodded.

Although Dr. Liu had already discovered through his pulse test the exact problem on Lloyd's left arm, he still asked him, "What ailment do you have?"

Lloyd said he had been in a traffic accident on the road, after which he could not raise his left arm, and now it had become disabled.

"Have you taken any medications or received any other treatments?" Dr. Liu continued.

"I have been taking Tylenol to relieve my pain," said Lloyd, too embarrassed to mention the other ineffective treatments he had received.

Lloyd's instinct told him Dr. Liu was a competent acupuncturist, so he changed his tone and said he had come for acupuncture treatment. Immediately, Dr. Liu showed him to one of his acupuncture beds and asked him to lie down.

Lloyd lay down, feeling relieved and relaxed, as he said to himself: *I don't need to apologize to him after all. He didn't even recognize me. But will acupuncture really work on me? Is it painful? Is it safe? Well, I may as well refrain from asking questions today, or I may embarrass him again. May God bless me! What should I do if acupuncture doesn't cure my pain? Oh, I'd better relax and cooperate with him since I am his patient. I always want my own patients to have confidence in me. When patients have confidence in their doctors, their conditions improve faster, so I should be a good, cooperative patient. Here he comes. He looks professional in his white gown, just like one of the mainstream doctors. He is carrying that small tray. It must be the tray where he puts his scary needles. From his airs, I can see he's got to be a good acupuncturist. At least, he looks like one.*

"Ready?" Dr. Liu came over, put down his tray on the end table, and then picked up his needles and alcohol swabs. He wiped the joint between Lloyd's left arm and shoulder with an alcohol swab, and then flicked a tiny needle into that point. Lloyd felt a painful, numb sensation when it went in, but he had an even stronger reaction when Dr. Liu manipulated the needle from side to side. Lloyd, a very sensitive person, nearly let out a cry, but a man wouldn't scream for such a thing, especially when his wife was around. He gritted his teeth and endured it quietly. He knew the needle itself was too small to cause such a strong reaction in his arm and that it could be a good sign, perhaps a signal of improvement.

Llyod was holding his breath for more needles, but Dr. Liu just covered him with a small blanket and said, "Relax and rest now."

Just this little needle? Lloyd was wondering. *Isn't he going to put more needles on my arms and elsewhere? Look. He walks away. So, just one single needle? Will it have any real effect on me? My other Canadian colleagues used all those heavy machines and expensive equipment, including their adept hands and nimble fingers, and none of it worked.*

Lloyd would shake his head if he could, but he realized he had decided to give acupuncture a chance. Therefore, he stopped worrying altogether. If it did not work, he would not come again anyway. Soon, he fell asleep.

"Did you fall asleep?" Dr. Liu woke him up about forty-five minutes later.

"Yes. I did." Lloyd opened his eyes, feeling energetic.

"You can get up and get dressed now," Dr. Liu said.

So, that's it? Lloyd said to himself. *One single needle and a nap? And that's it?*

Lloyd got up, using both hands, soon realizing that his condition had been cured. He lifted his right hand, then his left, then both to the same height. "Oh my God!" he screamed, as he became sure the single needle had cured his disabled arm that had tortured him for so many days and nights. "How is this possible?" The familiar pain and numbness were all gone.

His wife was scared when she heard him screaming and rushed toward the door of the acupuncture room, only to see him raising both hands high in the air. Lloyd still could not believe what had happened when he saw Karen smiling at him outside the door with her thumbs up.

"How do you feel now?" Dr. Liu asked him. "Raise your arm and see how you feel."

Lloyd did so, as if giving a demonstration to his own patients, saying, "Unbelievable!"

Dr. Liu looked pleased.

"Look, Karen!" Lloyd raised his left hand high up in the air again. "I've got back my arm and my hand!" He raised both arms repeatedly, just to convince himself that his disabled arm had really been cured.

"I can't believe it!" screamed Karen, who had been waiting for him the whole time. "Thank you so very much, Dr. Liu!" she said in tears. She had hoped for a miracle but had not expected it to happen so quickly.

"It's magical!" Lloyd said, as he looked at Dr. Liu gratefully. "Do I need to come again?"

"No—unless you have more pain, numbness, or stiffness," said Dr. Liu.

"How much should I pay you?" he asked, still in disbelief.

"One hundred dollars," said Dr. Liu.

"Wow! A single needle for one hundred dollars!" Lloyd said smilingly.

"Your arm is not even worth one hundred dollars?" Dr. Liu sounded quite serious.

"I was just joking, Dr. Liu," a shamefaced Lloyd chuckled. "One hundred dollars for this needle is really a very good deal. I truly appreciate it." Then, he beamed broadly, while Dr. Liu smiled, knowing it was not a complaint.

On their way home, Lloyd took the wheel instead. He thanked Karen for urging him to come and see Dr. Liu, still wondering why that single hair-like needle was able to cure his injury the other Canadian doctors could not. Which medical theory could explain it? Now he understood why Dr. Liu could not answer such questions to his satisfaction at the conference. Theory or no theory, at the end of the day, he got back his arm and his hand, and that was what really mattered.

A Real Doctor

"Dr. Liu, I cannot breathe. I am dying. Could you save me?" cried a woman on the phone. She had short breaths and was gasping for air. Dr. Liu was shocked by the severity of her symptoms.

"What's wrong with you?" he said sympathetically.

"I have SARS," she said chokingly. "No one likes me. They want to lock me up and leave me to die by myself."

"Come to my clinic immediately and I will do my best for you," he said.

"All the doctors have refused to see me," she said. "But aren't you afraid of death? If you see me, you may catch SARS and die too."

"If death has to take place, I am the doctor, I shall die first." Dr. Liu sounded so sincere, so caring, and so confident.

She thanked him in tears and was on her way at once.

Sarah Sweety, a 40-year-old French-speaking lady, was called "Sars" by her family, school friends, and colleagues in her office. Just on Monday, she had everything. She was living with her boyfriend; she had two loving parents; she was an accountant at the city's housing office. Overnight, she lost everything and everyone, including her name, which she had loved to hear until recently.

All Sars's trouble started in February, just about three months earlier, when a family that had visited Hong Kong returned to her city with the new life-threatening disease known as "severe acute respiratory syndrome," or "SARS," in short. This family went to the Scarborough Hospital for treatment, triggering an unstoppable spread of the virus that caused panic and death in the city. On March 26, the provincial government declared a state of emergency that allowed doctors and the government to take whatever action necessary to prevent the virus from spreading to other patients, health workers, and the general public.

On Tuesday morning, outside the hospital, Sars was notified by phone that she had tested SARS positive, and by law, she must quarantine. She had been coughing badly and had difficulty breathing. She was prepared for the worst, but she still nearly collapsed when she heard of the test results. She was haunted that being quarantined meant being locked up to die. Anyone who was infected with this incurable virus was treated like a public enemy, and no one would care about them whether they died of hunger, cold, or the disease.

Assuming no one else knew about her condition yet, she wanted to see her family physician to ask him to prescribe some medications for her, but he would not see her. When she called to make an appointment with him, she heard only a recorded message asking SARS patients to go to the nearby hospital instead. She didn't know what to do. She called the hospital and told them she had difficulty breathing and needed to go to the hospital but was told not to come because the few special wards with negative pressure were fully occupied, and there were already many patients on the waiting list. She called five other doctors, but they all refused to see her. Finally, she gave up.

Her boyfriend was the only one with whom she could share her misery now, so she called him and told him about her test results. During this conversation, she repeatedly requested that she be called Sarah instead of Sars from then on. She was hoping to hear some comforting words from him or at least some sympathetic understanding. Sarah said she wanted to see him in his apartment, but he told her, "In fact, I lost my key after you left my apartment, and I had to hire a locksmith to replace the lock on the door. He did it just half an hour ago. You can't even enter my apartment anymore. I can't see you today."

"Oh God! Can you drive me to my parents' home instead then?" she asked.

"Sars—oh, Sarah," he seemed to murmur to himself before he cleared his voice and said, "I'm so sorry, Sarah, I'm at the airport waiting to board the plane for New York at this moment. I am on an emergency business trip, and I won't be back for quite some time. I will call you when I return home."

Sarah was baffled, wondering why there was such a coincidence. The boyfriend who had trusted her all these years suddenly had to change his lock, and why was he taking an emergency business trip at this very moment when she needed him the most? She stood still on the pavement, as if her legs had been filled with cement.

The last hope she had was her parents, whom she had not visited since last Christmas. Her parents' home was on Kennedy Road near Sheppard Avenue. It was a 30-minute walk, but it took her an hour and a half to walk there. She knew she would be breaking the law if she took a taxi or a bus. She did not even think of taking one anyway. When she finally arrived at her parents' front porch and knocked on the door, they did not open it.

"Who is it?" her mother asked.

"Mom, it's Sarah. Oh, no, it's me, Sars."

"Oh, I hear you are sick," said her mother. "What brings you over at this moment?" She was just opening the door when she heard Sarah burst into an uncontrollable cough. "You're really sick, Sars, aren't you?"

"Mom, I've got SARS!" She burst into sobs while coughing.

"What?" cried her mother. She quickly shut the door she had been opening. "Go to the hospital right now! We can't let you in."

"I can't even see a doctor. No doctors want to see me. No hospital wants to take me. My boyfriend has changed his lock and I cannot get into his apartment." Sarah continued sobbing helplessly.

"Wait a minute," said her mother behind the door. "I know an acupuncturist who is pretty good. Try your luck and see if he is willing to see you."

"But," said Sarah. "Can acupuncture cure a deadly virus?"

"I don't know, but here is his contact information. His name is Dr. Wan Cheng Liu. His phone number is 9299—I forget the rest. Anyway, you can find it yourself online. Then, just add the area code. Go see him now. Good luck, Sars."

"Please, Mom. Don't call me Sars anymore. Call me Sarah!"

"Okay, my dear! Good luck!"

Hoping against hope, before contacting Dr. Liu, Sarah called the manager of the housing office for assistance but was told, "In accordance with the Health Protection and Promotion Act, you cannot return to work until the government health official allows you to. Please take care of yourself."

Outside her parents' home, Sarah felt she was left to die in the cold in this once warm city. She could not see a doctor and had no medications for her illness. She had no place to live and no food to eat. Suicide flashed across her mind. The only glimpse of hope she had was an unknown acupuncturist. She pulled herself together and tried to call him.

Toronto had two area codes: 416, the older one, and 647, a newer one. She assumed that Dr. Liu's phone number contained the latter, which was the case. She added it to the incomplete number her mother had given her. Then, she tried to call him, by adding three numbers at a time until she accidentally got through to him after her third attempt.

Then came the dialogue in the beginning of the story.

At 1:00 p.m., Sarah, who was running a high fever and struggling with her breathing, was lying on Dr. Liu's acupuncture bed receiving his treatment. He flicked the hair-like silvery needles into the acupuncture points on her head, hands, legs, and elsewhere. Soon her breathing began to improve, and then she fell asleep. Her first treatment lasted an hour. After Dr. Liu removed her needles, she got up, feeling her body had been recharged with energy. She felt warm and strong. Then, Dr. Liu also prescribed some Chinese herbal medications for her, which she was asked to mix with boiling water and take orally three times daily. Three days later, under his meticulous medical care, Sarah started to recover; her sore throat, her uncontrollable cough, her fever all improved rapidly.

She came for further treatment once daily for nine more days. Then, Dr. Liu declared she had fully recovered. Sarah seemed to have woken up from a dream, or rather a nightmare, but it was such a heart-warming feeling.

What Sarah did not know was that Dr. Liu had caught the SARS virus from her. When he was giving her the first treatment, he felt a pungent odor released from her lungs striking his nostrils. Like other healthcare professionals, Dr. Liu was not well prepared for the SARS virus, and he did not wear a mask. He did not even have one, for he had never worn one when treating patients. Half an hour after she left his clinic, Dr. Liu's nose started running. Then, it became stuffy, and soon, he could hardly breathe through it. These were unmistakable early SARS symptoms. He immediately gave himself acupuncture treatment and herbal medications at the same time. He flicked acupuncture needles into his own acupoints to boost up his immunity and then consolidated the efficacy with a hot dose of herbal medicine. Despite this, he still ran a low fever the next day, which lasted for a day and a half. He would give himself acupuncture treatment and take his herbal medication following each of Sarah's subsequent visits. Dr. Liu's symptoms disappeared three days later. After twelve days of treatment, Sarah also fully recovered from SARS without sequelae.

"Dr. Liu, you are a real doctor!" Sarah sobbed when she heard of her recovery.

Dr. Liu grinned, not knowing what "a real doctor" really

meant.

"You are not afraid of death!" she continued.

"You are my patient," said Dr. Liu. "Saving my patient's life is my job. As I said before, if one of us has to die, I shall go first." He looked at her caringly.

Sarah threw herself into his arms, not knowing what to say anymore. After a long silence, she said, "I owe my life to you."

Be a Real Woman Again

Thirty-year-old Eliza Haimukaier burst into uncontrollable sobs when her doctor showed her the hysteroscopy reports and told her that her only option was a hysterectomy, or complete removal of her uterus. The young woman, who was known as a sunshine girl from kindergarten to high school, felt as if she had been struck by a thunderbolt, unable to suppress her emotions in front of the doctor.

Eliza had started to show menstrual-disorder symptoms more than two years earlier. In one month, her five-day menstruation lasted nine days instead, and the next month, ten days, and then, twelve days, until she knew something was wrong with her. She looked feeble and fragile and had faint pain in her lower abdomen. Three months earlier, she had started seeking help from her doctors. She ended up seeing a gynecologist in the hospital for a thorough examination of her uterus. Today, she had come for the sentencing from the specialist, knowing his announcement of her hysteroscopy results would not be a friendly one.

He had just gone through the details with her: she had more than twenty uterine fibroids, large ones and small ones that covered the uterine walls. The largest one was 5.5 cm. Since there was no effective medicine for fibroids, and she had so many of them, she could only have them surgically removed, which meant complete removal of her womb. Otherwise, her condition would deteriorate, and she would eventually die of uterine hemorrhage.

She dragged her feet out of the doctor's office. She did not know how to break the news to her husband, who was waiting for her in the waiting room.

"Eliza, what did the doctor say?" he asked, anxious about the results of her hysteroscopy.

What did he say? she said to herself. *He said too much! Do you really want to know what he said?! Your wife will lose her entire womb. A woman, a wife without a womb! That's what he said. Your wife won't be a woman anymore. What would you say to that? Do you want to keep a woman without a womb? My poor man does not know my real condition, but he has seen tears in my eyes, and he knows the doctor has said something bad. Should I tell him the truth or a lie? Should I let him find out in bed that I have lost my womb after my surgery? What good would there be then? But if I tell him now, can he take it? Would he divorce me right away? But Eliza, think of it this way: you can't expect a young husband to keep a wife without a womb. It is unreasonable just to hope for or pray for a normal relationship if you don't even have a womb. A woman without a womb is just like a man without a penis. Would you have married a man without a penis? I love him. I want him to be happy. He loves me. He wants me to be happy, too. Or should I simply take my own life to free him? Or should I divorce him instead and let him find another woman? Love or no love, I will find out whether he loves me. I will just tell him the truth and let him decide.*

"Ryan," Eliza said calmly after her long silence, looking into his eyes. "It is bad news for me, and it is bad news for you too."

"What did the doctor say?" He raised his hands to wipe the tears on her face, his heart throbbing with anxiety.

"Since you really want to know, I will just tell you the truth," said Eliza, as she cleared her voice. "Then, you will make your decision. I love you and I don't mind."

"Come on! I am listening," he said eagerly.

"I have uterine fibroids, or tumors in the womb," she uttered word by word. "The doctor says the only cure is surgery."

"Surgery?"

"Yes," she said, as she stared at him. "Complete removal of my entire womb!"

"Did he tell you any other options?" he asked.

"Nope!" said Eliza. "He is the best specialist in Budapest. He has done numerous surgeries for women with the same problem."

"Don't panic, Eliza. There must be some other options," said Ryan after recovering from his shock.

"Your wife will have no womb, Ryan. Let's divorce so that you can find another woman and remarry," said Eliza.

"Silly girl! Don't you ever think of leaving me," Ryan said in a stern voice. "I won't let you go, not for women or wealth! Listen, you are my only wife and last wife. Period! Please, don't ever scare me again. I just can't stand it. I don't mind if you really have to lose your womb."

"I am serious, Ryan," Eliza said.

"Let's go home. You may find alternative treatment. You never know." He grabbed her hand, and they left the waiting room.

No sooner had they arrived home than Ryan started calling relatives, friends, acquaintances, and colleagues to inquire about doctors who could cure uterine fibroids without surgery. Meanwhile, he also looked through advertisements posted by doctors and other healthcare professionals in newspapers and magazines. The result was that, by 5:00 p.m., he had found an acupuncturist by the name of Wan Cheng Liu, who had, without surgery and medications, cured many women's uterine fibroids, using only acupuncture needles. Dr. Liu's success rate was over 97%, including 34% full recovery and 63% showing significant improvement. As reported in one study, the uncured or incompletely cured cases were mostly attributed to patients' inability to continue with their treatments, either because they could not afford them or they had to move away from the city. Ryan became so hopeful that happy tears streamed down his cheeks. "God's will!" he said to himself. He knew his wife's fibroids would be cured even before seeing Dr. Liu.

Ryan broke the good news to Eliza, who was deeply touched by his tireless search that led to their successful contact with the genius acupuncturist from China who had been treating patients in Budapest. Without delay, they booked the earliest appointment available with Dr. Liu.

Eliza went to see Dr. Liu the following morning. He diagnosed her, calmed her down, wanted her to have confidence in herself, and asked for her full cooperation. That is, he wanted her to never think of divorce and suicide. Then, he wanted her to come for treatment as he prescribed to achieve the best efficacy. For love, for her husband and their marriage, for the pride of womanhood, she promised full cooperation with the doctor. She had her first treatment on the same trip.

For love, for her husband and their marriage, Eliza went for fifty treatments, once daily. Dr. Liu's miraculous treatment was brought into full play. Eliza soon learned that the genius acupuncturist was worthy of every title he had and was just as good as described in every success story published in newspapers, magazines, and books; seen on TV; and heard through word of mouth. After her fiftieth treatment, she went back to her gynecologist in the hospital, who prescribed another hysteroscopy for her. The results stunned the gynecologist and left him wondering how Dr. Liu's tiny needles were able to cure all her uterine fibroids.

The grateful couple returned to Dr. Liu for the last time, not for further treatment, but to express their heartfelt thanks to him. They had brought him the best gift they could find in Budapest's best gift store, not knowing what Dr. Liu appreciated the most was Eliza's last tearful words: "Dr. Liu, you have given me a chance to be a 'real woman' again!"

Secret Visits

Geo was the head of the Quality Control Lab of the city's water plant. He had a BA in physics and an MA in chemistry. For everything he did, he would look for a scientific theory to explain it. If he could not find one, he just would not believe it. For this reason, he often clashed with his wife, Annie, who was a college graduate and who believed in end results instead of science theories and formulas.

Lately, their conflicts escalated because of their beliefs in medicine. Geo would see only doctors of conventional medicine, whether their treatment was effective or not. At least these doctors could explain every condition in clear terms that he could understand. For him, if something was not curable because of the doctor's limited medical knowledge, he would understand it and accept it. For this reason, at times Geo found Annie annoying.

In his mind, she did not seem to appreciate the free healthcare in Canada, and when an illness was incurable or had no effective cure, she would still dream of finding a cure. She would not hesitate to pay out of her own pocket for alternative treatment, like traditional Chinese medicine, especially acupuncture, which Geo thought was not science because no science theory could explain it clearly. To him, acupuncture was no different from superstition, spiritual healing, and witchcraft. Despite all this, Geo forgave her most of the time, thinking that he was better educated, especially in hard science, while Annie had only a college education, and her English was not good enough, at least, not up to the level of a juror candidate.

"Annie, you have an appointment with the hepatologist tomorrow," he said to her at breakfast on April 25.

"Oh, do I?" she asked. "How come I didn't know?"

"I'm sorry. I must have forgotten to tell you about this appointment," he apologized. "I thought you might have difficulty communicating with the doctor's assistant, so I made the appointment for you half a year ago."

Geo was expecting a thank-you from her, but she did not give him one. More disappointing still, she did not seem to appreciate it.

"Geo," said Annie after a moment of silence, "I would rather not go, if you don't mind."

"Why? The cyst on your liver is getting bigger and bigger," he said. "You need to get the proper treatment and try to bring it under control without delay."

"Come on, Geo. You know I have been seeing the specialist for three years," Annie said calmly. "The cyst used to be smaller than 1 cm, but the last X-ray shows it had become ten or fifteen times as big. If he was able to cure it or control it, it shouldn't have grown to the present size."

"Annie, you can't expect the specialist to be able to cure every disease. Some diseases are curable, and some are not. Some take more time to cure than others." He wanted to cite more scientific reasons but soon realized Annie was not interested, so he cut himself short, repeating what he had said previously, "You need to cooperate with the hepatologist."

"I would rather not go this time. Really, Geo." She sounded very stubborn and determined, which really upset him now.

"What's the problem with you, Annie?"

"I think my cyst probably has gone, or at least it must have shrunk a lot, Geo."

"What!" he cried. "How could it be? You just don't believe in science. It is simple physics. It is simple chemistry. You didn't have surgery; you have not taken any medications; you have been eating the same food and doing the same work every day. How could it suddenly become smaller? And how could it possibly disappear? How I wish it did!"

"Geo, I know you studied science and you want to apply physics and chemistry theories in everything you do," said Annie. "I respect you for that, but today, I must tell you something, which you may not want to believe."

"You won't tell me about alternative medicine, will you?"

"I will," Annie said. "That's exactly what I wish to tell you. I need your patience today. I just want five minutes from you."

"Oh God! Alternative medicine again!" He shook his head, sighing helplessly, but he restrained himself from further escalation.

Annie told him she had been receiving acupuncture treatment from a genius specialist who had cured or effectively controlled more than one of her conditions. She began by asking for Geo's forgiveness and understanding for not letting him know about her "secret" acupuncture treatment, the primary reason of which was his stubborn objection and repeated denial of alternative medicine. Then, she unfolded her stories that shocked him.

"Geo, I don't deny that our mainstream medicine is among the best in the world. The doctors and nurses are all extremely well trained and they are competent and committed to their profession. It is they who treat and cure most of the illnesses of the population. Healthcare is one of the reasons why we live in Canada, and one that we are proud of, but as you said, not every doctor can cure every disease of every patient, and neither can any type of medicine, be it conventional medicine or traditional Chinese medicine. But you need to believe my stories today." She paused, looking into Geo's eyes. By now he had calmed down.

"I am listening," he said, frowning. "Just continue anyway."

"Geo, after I learned that my cyst had grown to 10 cm, I became scared. Then, I started searching for alternative treatment. Fortunately, I found Dr. Liu, a real acupuncturist who knows what he is doing and who does the impossible for many of his patients. Almost every one of his patients I have met has one ailment or another that our mainstream doctors cannot cure. That is why they come to him, which means paying for their alternative treatment out of their own pocket, unless they have an extended healthcare plan that covers acupuncture."

"Go on," Geo said. "I'm waiting to hear MIRACLES!"

"Geo, indeed, MIRACLES! I am not joking! The past six months was an eventful period for me. I had so many health issues. You know about my liver cyst, but I did not tell you about my kidney cysts, and you did not even know who cured my unbearable, painful shingles."

"You have kept so many secrets from me!" he protested.

"Geo, I want you to understand why I could not tell you earlier. It is all because of your stubborn objection to alternative treatment. If I had told you what I wanted to do, I might not have had any of my ailments cured by the acupuncturist, won't you agree?"

"Oh God!" he complained. "Everything I have been doing is for you, for your good, to protect you!"

"Anyway, Geo, to cut the long story short, I started seeing Dr. Liu five months ago. After the first acupuncture treatment, I felt something was changing inside me. I felt energetic, strong, and warm even on a cold winter day. Before long, the discomfort in my liver area disappeared. I used to feel it after eating a full meal. Now, it is all gone."

"What did Dr. Liu use to rid of your trouble?" Geo asked.

"Several tiny needles, not much bigger than a hair."

"Is that all?" he questioned.

"No kidding, Geo. As recommended by my family doctor, I had another X-ray taken after the treatment, and the reports showed the liver cyst had disappeared!"

"I hope you are not advertising for Dr. Liu!" he laughed

bitterly.

"Geo, don't forget, I also had kidney cysts. The largest one was 4.4 cm," said Annie. "You can read my lab reports for yourself. I wish I had told Dr. Liu about them when I asked him to treat my liver cyst, but I did not. Now that I had seen such a miracle happening after the twenty treatments, I asked him if he could also cure my kidney cysts. He said they were curable, or at the very least he could shrink them and help me control them."

"And did he really try?" asked Geo.

"Yes, he did," Annie said. "After I rested for a week, I started my second period of treatment with Dr. Liu, who directly targeted my kidney cysts. Honestly, it was effective but not perfect treatment. After thirty treatments, all my smaller kidney cysts were gone, and the largest one had unbelievably shrunk from 4.4 cm to 1 cm, as my last ultrasound examination showed. Now I do not feel the numbness and pain on my back or any other discomfort around the kidney area anymore. I owe everything to Dr. Liu."

"I would be overjoyed if my wife has recovered from these serious ailments!" Geo's face lit up.

"Geo, you still remember taking me to the hospital for emergency treatment for my unendurable shingles early last month, don't you?"

"Very clearly," said Geo. "I also bought the medicine for you. You took it and you soon recovered."

"But that was not the case. You bought the medicine the doctor had prescribed for me, but I did not take it. By that time, I really trusted Dr. Liu, so I went to see him after I left the hospital and showed him the medication."

"What did Dr. Liu say then?" asked Geo.

"Geo, Dr. Liu said it was the wrong medicine. It would not cure my shingles. Just like asking for a star from the sky, I carelessly said, 'Can acupuncture cure shingles?' He said, 'Yes, of course. It is even more effective than the medicine you have.'

I don't mean to say I did not trust him, but I also found it very difficult to believe. But since acupuncture had no side effects and I already had satisfactory results from my previous treatments, I decided to try acupuncture treatment for my shingles as well."

"And?" Geo raised his head and fixed his eyes on Annie.

"Geo, believe it or not! It took two treatments, each less than an hour. And my unbearably painful shingles were thoroughly cured. I asked Dr. Liu why his acupuncture treatment was so effective—even better than antibiotics. He said because I came early—before the blisters broke. I had thought that with the unbroken blisters, the water or toxic stuff, whatever it is called, was still inside, it would be more difficult to cure, but I thanked God for letting me choose Dr. Liu and his treatment."

"I hope you are not writing science fiction, Annie. Can you tell me Dr. Liu's phone number and address? I need to see him in person to believe such an angel really exists on earth."

"Geo, here," said Annie, giving him a business card. "It's Dr. Liu's business card. His contact info is all here."

"Wait a minute," Geo cut her short. "Can I see the reports he has given to you?"

"He has never given me any reports," she said uneasily, "so I have nothing to show you."

"I do want to believe you, Annie," said Geo, "but how can I? I need something better than your own vivid descriptions."

"Geo, tell me. How do you want me to prove to you what I have said is true?" said the helpless wife.

"Could you see the hepatologist as scheduled tomorrow? Tell him what you have told me and ask him for another ultrasound examination of your liver and kidneys."

"Geo, for this reason, I would be more than delighted to go," beamed Annie, nodding her head in confidence.

The next morning saw Annie repeating her stories to the hepatologist, who prescribed another ultrasound examination for a double purpose: to monitor the changes in her conditions and to satisfy her request. As Annie had confidently expected, the ultrasound reports came within a week, confirming that her liver cyst was not found and that all her kidney cysts had disappeared except the largest one that had shrunk from 4.4 cm to 1 cm.

The overjoyed husband, who had got back a healthy wife in such a strange way, was still in disbelief. He asked the hepatologist for an explanation of his wife's acupuncture cure but got none. When he got home, he called Dr. Liu for his acupuncture theory but received no satisfactory answer. All he knew was that Annie had become a healthy person, and he finally realized there were so many things that could not be explained by physics and chemistry theories. Or rather, these theories just could not explain everything on earth or in the universe.

At the end of the day, what really mattered was Annie became a healthier wife and he became a happier husband. In his heart he was grateful to Dr. Liu for his miraculous treatments.

"My Last Doctor"

She carelessly stepped into the Acupuncture Clinic, agitated and depressed.

"You are Dr. Liu?" She started talking when the doctor raised his head.

"Yes. What can I do for you?" Dr. Liu glanced at her. She looked like a withered flower, showing signs of fatigue and anxiety. Her eyes were dull, covered with red webs; her hair was messy with tangled knots, though it seemed to have been combed. She neither showed the same respect other patients had for the doctor nor appeared to expect anything from her visit.

"You are my last doctor," she said.

"Your last doctor? What do you mean?" Dr. Liu said to himself.

"I'm Lyndia. I have an appointment with you for acupuncture treatment," she said.

"Sure. Sit down here, please," he said, pointing at the patient's chair on the other side of his diagnosis table.

"This is the last time I am going to try treatment," she said mysteriously. "You are my last doctor," she repeated dryly.

"Well?" Dr. Liu's face became a question mark. He asked her to place her wrist on the wrist cushion before he began the standard diagnostic procedure. He felt her pulse, while she kept talking

"I have been suffering from insomnia. It has been torturing me for five years. In the beginning I took one sleeping pill before going to bed; then I took two, and then three, but in vain.

I have seen two Canadian experts and three doctors of traditional Chinese medicine. I took Western medications and Chinese herbal medications at the same time while I was receiving acupuncture from another practitioner. None of them did me any good. Instead, my trouble is getting worse and worse."

"I see," said Doctor Liu, who had completed her pulse test.

"There is a bridge over the highway on my way here. I almost jumped off the bridge to finish my sufferings. But I thought I would give myself one last chance. You are my last doctor. If you cannot cure my illness, I will take my own life." She sounded determined.

Dr. Liu took it seriously, saying, "Then, I don't want to be your doctor."

"Why not?" she said, surprised.

"It's unfair," he said. "You have seen five other doctors, and none of them has cured your illness. I am the sixth one. If I cannot cure you and if you kill yourself, won't it be unfair for me?"

"But it's my own decision," she said. "There's nothing to do with you."

"You are wrong," said Dr. Liu. "If you really took your own life, people would think I had caused your death. Wouldn't you make me feel and look like a killer? Wouldn't you make me feel guilty for the rest of my life?"

"Doctor Liu, you don't know how miserable I am! For me, every day is a day of stress and anxiety, a day of pain and suffering, a day of torture. I cannot sleep at all, day or night. I cannot work, I cannot get along with my family. I lose my temper all the time, often for no reason. My relationship with my husband is very tense."

"How old are you?"

"Forty-four. For me, life is no fun. My stubborn insomnia has caused me problems all over the body: ear ringing, severe headache, tense and painful muscles, and the list goes on.

Death will relieve me from all my sufferings. I really cannot stand it anymore," she sobbed.

"But insomnia is curable," said Dr. Liu.

"The other doctors told me the same thing, but none of them cured me. To be honest with you, I don't trust doctors anymore," she said. "I haven't been able to sleep for many days and months. I just cannot sleep. I cannot work. I cannot live. I am sad. I am miserable. Life is meaningless for me." She paused, then looked at Dr. Liu hesitantly and said, "Can you really cure my insomnia?"

"Yes. But you must have confidence in yourself, and you must cooperate with me," he assured her.

"How do I cooperate?" she said.

"First of all, you must never again think about taking your own life. Then, you need to be patient and give me a chance. Come for a full period of treatment, once a day."

"How long do I need to come?" She was eager to know.

"We will try twelve days first and see what happens."

"How much do you charge for each treatment?" She was wondering if the doctor would charge a fortune to save her life.

Dr. Liu told her the cost of each treatment and then added, "It's the same rate for everyone."

She nodded, indicating she was willing to try Dr. Liu's treatment. "When can I start?"

"Right now," he said, showing her to the acupuncture room. "Lie on here and relax." Then, he went over to his desk at the corner and soon came back with his needle tray. He bent over and flicked seven or eight hair-like needles into her head and other acupoints elsewhere.

For someone who has never seen this, it may look rather scary; you may even wonder if the needles would touch the brain underneath, but Dr. Liu knows every one of these acupoints and he knows exactly where to insert his needles.

"Relax and try to sleep, if you can," Dr. Liu said. Then, he closed the door gently for her to rest. About forty minutes later, he returned to check on her. To his happy surprise, she was asleep. "That's a good sign," he said to himself.

For this patient, it was a matter of life and death, so Dr. Liu did not wake her up, though the regular treatment was over. Instead, he let her sleep, but he kept the door half-open so that he could hear her when she woke up.

"What time is it, Doctor Liu?" she called when she finally woke up.

"It's five o'clock," he said, looking at his watch. "You have been sleeping for quite a while, haven't—"

"Oh, have I?" she interrupted. Dr. Liu could see joy and happiness spilling out of her face and hear the calmness from her voice and words.

"You can get up and go home now," said Dr. Liu after removing all her needles. "Come back at the same time tomorrow," he told her.

When she returned the next day, she told Dr. Liu, "I felt really sleepy when I got home yesterday. And I soundly slept for more than two hours last night. It was the longest and best sleep I ever had during the past few years."

She was excited to receive the second treatment, then the third, and then the fourth. She fully cooperated with Dr. Liu, and after twelve days of treatment, she was able to sleep for five to six hours, but during this first course of treatment, she also had days when she almost wanted to give up. Fortunately, Dr. Liu always encouraged her to continue with her treatment. That is why she was able to experience such positive results as a 5- to 6-hour daily sleep in the end.

By now she realized that full recovery might require a total of thirty treatments, and she was mentally prepared for that. She was so grateful to Dr. Liu that she wrote a letter in appreciation of his miraculous treatment and had it published in a newspaper in Toronto. Not only was she in a mood to write a letter to the newspaper, but she even joked with her husband, "You won't have a chance to see a snapped string on the guitar anymore, because I can continue to live my life now." She apologized to her family for all her rude behavior in the past when she constantly yelled at them for no reason.

"My husband, who did not believe in Chinese medicine has become a true believer now," she said. "My gratitude toward Dr. Liu is beyond words. He is worthy of the titles 'PhD' and 'Professor.' He is a rare genius in acupuncture. Literally, he saved my life."

Miraculous Height Increase

It is my pleasure to share with you my son's successful acupuncture treatment story.

Talking about my son, I always feel overwhelmed whenever I recall what we had experienced prior to seeking treatment from Dr. Liu. Our experience cannot be described in a few words, so I beg your patience. But before telling you about the details of his acupuncture story, I would like to brief you on his previous condition.

Straight to the point, my son's acupuncture treatment by Dr. Liu was God's blessing. We were just so very fortunate. As you may well guess, like other mothers, I love my son dearly and expect much of him. He is part of me, part of my life. He is everything in the family. Needless to say, I wanted him to grow like other boys, to be a healthy, happy man and be accepted by his peers.

But in 2006, when Charlie was nearly seventeen years old, my hope simply became a wish that would not come true. The endocrinologist at SickKids Hospital dropped a bombshell on my family, announcing that my once healthy child had a condition called hypothyroidism.

Theoretically, mild cases of hypothyroidism are treatable, and severe ones are controllable, though it means a lifetime of medication. Common treatment, as popularly known, is adjusting the amount of thyroid hormone to meet the body's demand, or in extreme cases, simply replacing it. The doctors at SickKids, including the endocrinologist, lost no time in prescribing treatments for him. They did everything they could to improve his condition. Charlie had one test after another and was given treatment after treatment, which all had proven effectiveness for most patients.

To our dismay, not only did they fail to improve Charlie's condition after two years of continuous testing and treatments, but during these two years, he stopped growing altogether. At the age of nearly nineteen, his height and weight were far from the average of boys of his age, measuring only 5'4" and 126 pounds.

If your son or daughter has stopped growing for two or three years, at the age of nineteen, they may never grow again. It became clear to us that if Charlie's condition did not improve, he would not continue to grow or meet the average weight and height for his age. At this point my husband and I realized that, despite all the great doctors, labs, and medications, conventional medical practices were no longer an option for him.

We were devastated! Just devastated!

My average expectations of a son were crushed instantly at this moment of realization: my son had stopped growing and would remain a severely underweight and abnormally short man! Alternative medicine was the only hope we had. Then, we thought of our acupuncturist, Dr. Liu, a genius acupuncturist who had cured many diseases declared incurable by mainstream doctors and hospitals.

In fact, I had known him for seven years. He had successfully treated various ailments of my family, including urinary tract infections, menopause symptoms, dry eyes and other related problems, but could acupuncture cure hypothyroidism? Could he increase my son's height and weight? We turned to him without further delay.

"Yes," Dr. Liu said, "hypothyroidism is a curable disease." Dr. Liu gave us hope, assuring us that Charlie would continue to grow with acupuncture treatment. It would require daily treatment for a prescribed period, the exact length depending on how fast his condition improved.

Thank God! We were about to see light at the end of the tunnel!

Experiencing is believing! Charlie started his first treatment on the day he saw Dr. Liu, and he continued to receive his daily treatment for three months. After each treatment every day, he not only felt good physically but also mentally. His condition improved noticeably in the absence of conventional medicine, until it was cured. After the three-month treatment, we measured Charlie's weight and height. He had grown two inches and gained ten pounds, becoming a man of 5'6" and 136 pounds.

What a miracle! It was a miracle created by a miracle doctor!

I was astounded at the unbelievable results, tears gushing down my cheeks. It was not just the physical results, but the emotional improvement was just as important. The timely treatment had not just increased Charlie's energy level and given him more confidence that made him a much happier person, but it had also lifted a weight from my heart and made me a stress-free mother. Charlie had grown to be taller than Dr. Liu. He had become a tall, handsome young man, ready for dating, ready for starting his own life.

By the way, I have also read about another patient, a 19-year-old lady from Hong Kong who, in her letter of appreciation written to Dr. Liu in 2011, called it "an absolute astonishment" after he regulated her chronically irregular menstrual cycles with just three or four treatments and then increased her height by an unbelievable inch upon completion of her twenty treatments.

My dear friend, Dr. Liu knows more details about the changes that took place during my son's treatment and the treatment of the young lady from Hong Kong. If you want more information, you could contact him directly.

All I can tell you is that Dr. Liu is a miracle! I cannot find another word that can describe him more accurately. In my heart, I believe he is the only doctor in the world who can deliver these unbelievable results.

It's a Miracle

Mr. Young heard a horrible crash inside the living room. He rushed in only to find his wife lying motionless on the floor. She appeared to have suffered acute facial palsy. He was shocked at seeing her mouth badly twisted to one side and her fully exposed lower inner eyelid, known as ectropion. Her eye that could no longer move was fixed on him when he looked at her. He shivered as he asked her what had happened, but she did not respond. She had lost her memory and ability to speak.

The devastated husband was trembling, his mind all blank, but he managed to connect with 911. Though he was well known for his competency and efficiency, he was at a complete loss and struggling desperately to cope with the crisis. Only when the ambulance finally arrived and took his wife away did he breathe a sigh of relief.

Toronto has some of the world's best hospitals, and the doctors, especially the specialists of various diseases, are all well-trained experts, he thought, confident that they would rescue his wife.

But he was soon struck with another thunderbolt—the chief physician showed him the diagnosis reports, telling him that his wife had suffered a stroke and had become partially paralyzed. She was no longer the healthy wife he had seen early in the evening.

He nearly fainted, appealing to the doctor to rescue her. Doubtless, the doctor would do his best to cure her. Though the doctor did not sound very confident, Mr. Young still thought that his wife would recover from her stroke, but the doctor had a more devastating warning for him yet.

"I hate to tell you this, Mr. Young, but there is a high chance that your wife may suffer massive bleeding into the brain tissue, known as intracerebral hemorrhage, within the next ten days. If that happens, she may die."

Mr. Young nearly fainted again at the last warning, his ears starting ringing as his brain stopped working altogether. He could not hear anything from the doctor anymore. He stared at him blankly. Only his silence seemed to be communicating with the dejected doctor, who just lowered his head and walked away.

Mr. Young was distraught and disappointed at the same time. Distraught because his wife had suffered such a severe stroke at such a young age, while strokes usually struck seniors. Disappointed because it looked like such a great healthcare system with so many well-trained specialists could not even save his wife. He felt he was simply left there to wait for his wife to die.

In desperation, Mr. Young, who was also open to alternative medicine, thought of traditional Chinese medicine. "True or not, some people say conventional medicine provides accurate diagnosis but often offers no cure, while traditional Chinese medicine provides the most ambiguous diagnosis but often cures what Western medicine cannot," he said to himself. "Personally I know of quite a few cases where Chinese medicine has cured the 'incurable.'" He decided to seek alternative medical treatment for his wife without delay.

He thought of two options. "One is finding a herbal specialist, but herbal medicine requires my wife to take it orally, which is not only hard for her, but it may cause some side effects, or it may be subject to accusations of causing side effects to the patient by the doctors in the hospital. No, it's not the best choice. Another option is acupuncture. It is safe, and there are no medications to take. Therefore, it is difficult for any doctors and nurses in the hospital to blame the acupuncturist even if it is not effective. The question is, can the tiny needles save my wife? If so, which acupuncturist can I trust? Anyway, doing something is better than doing nothing. I just can't sit idly waiting for my wife to die."

He started looking for advertisements posted by alternative medical practitioners in Toronto. He also called friends and relatives, including those in Hong Kong, determined to find a competent acupuncturist to save his better half. He told them, "Saving my wife means saving my children's happy life and my own."

Mr. Young's frantic search ended with Dr. Wan Cheng Liu, PhD in acupuncture, who was the inventor of the flick-insertion acu-treatment method. Dr. Liu told him his wife could be saved and that subsequent hemorrhage in the brain could be prevented and that she also had a good chance of recovery.

Mr. Young felt a heavy weight was lifted from his heart, albeit temporarily, but he was faced with another dilemma. The hospital would not let him bring in Dr. Liu, who said he could save his wife. He had to choose between Dr. Liu, a lone acupuncturist, and the hospital, which could mean death for his wife.

"You cannot have it both ways," Dr. Liu told him. "You either choose my treatment and let me look after your wife and save her life, or you let the doctors in the hospital take care of her and wait for her possible death as they have warned you."

The heartbroken husband did not want to offend the doctors in the hospital and did not want to lose his wife, but he finally chose Dr. Liu. The arrangement was for Dr. Liu to treat her until she was released from the hospital, and then she would continue to receive acupuncture treatment from him.

Securing permission from the hospital to bring in Dr. Liu was no easy job. In the beginning, her conventional doctor was not enthusiastic and supportive, because he did not believe acupuncture would improve her condition, but Mr. Young had made up his mind. He insisted until the doctor had to agree.

"But you have to sign another Hospital Liability Waiver, and both you and the acupuncturist also have to sign other documents to release the hospital of all liability of your wife's death and any other unexpected incidents, should anything happen," said the hospital doctor. "In other words, if she unfortunately dies as a result of the acupuncture treatment, it is yours and the acupuncturist's sole responsibility." His warning went on, but it did not deter Mr. Young.

He called Dr. Liu and told him about all the documents they had to sign with the hospital. To his relief, Dr. Liu was not afraid. He had confidence in himself and the patient and readily accepted the challenge. To be brief, Dr. Liu and Mr. Young signed every legal document as required, which finally brought Dr. Liu to Mrs. Young's ward.

"Massive intracerebral hemorrhage can be prevented by acupuncture," Dr. Liu repeated to Mr. Young, in the presence of the hospital doctor.

Mr. Young was moved to tears. This was the first time he felt he was about to see a glimpse of light at the end of a long tunnel. He knew acupuncture was expensive, especially hiring a world-renowned expert who had to leave his clinic and travel back and forth to treat his wife. Each treatment would take Dr. Liu four hours, including travel time.

"Money is not a problem for me, Dr. Liu," he assured him. "I will do everything I have to do to save my wife's life. I will sell our house to pay for her treatment."

"Selling your house is not necessary," said Dr. Liu. "What's more important is you must have confidence and cooperate with me fully."

Tears welled up in Mr. Young's eyes. He was so grateful that he could keep his house. He had two girls aged two and four who needed a mother and a place to live in. He dared not imagine what would happen to them if they lost their mother, nor could he imagine a homeless life for them, his unhealthy wife, and himself. He promised to cooperate with Dr. Liu.

Mr. Young and his wife, both from Hong Kong, belonged to the super-immigrant category: university-educated in their thirties with excellent English proficiency. Mr. Young was a computer-engineering consultant, and his wife, a programmer. Like many other new Canadians in Toronto, they worked tirelessly to pay their mortgage and raise their children. Programming was a demanding job that required accuracy and, in turn, full attention. Mrs. Young not only worked hard in her office, but she regularly brought home extra work to complete at night.

It was just another usual Thursday evening in April for Mrs. Young. She put the two young children to sleep at about 9:30; then she continued with her programming, which she had not finished in the office, but five minutes later, she suffered her devastating stroke.

Before making his trip to the hospital, Dr. Liu went to the Chinese herbal drugstores downtown with Mr. Young to buy some Chinese herbal medicinal pills, the size of a small yolk sealed inside a wax ball. His wife would need them in the first week of Dr. Liu's care.

Mrs. Young's acupuncture treatment started without delay, with the hospital closely watching everything the acupuncturist was doing and monitoring her improvement after each treatment. For the first four weeks, she received her treatment once daily, after which she had it every other day. In the third month, Mrs. Young was released from the hospital.

The chief physician and the nurses were astounded that Dr. Liu's first treatment magically restored 70% of the patient's speech ability. Her daily improvement was monitored, verified, and recorded by the hospital using sophisticated equipment. It thoroughly proved Dr. Liu's acupuncture efficacy for his patient, which would not have been recorded if she were treated in his clinic. They turned it into undisputable "science." They were truly impressed by Dr. Liu's acupuncture treatment results and amazed by Mrs. Young's rapid recovery. The chief physician had finally come to respect Dr. Liu and appreciate his unbelievable treatment.

"It's a miracle! A miracle from God!" he said to Mrs. Young on the day she was discharged from the hospital.

Problem with the Triplets

Before him is a large, tall baby stroller with two lovely baby twins sitting side by side in the front. The stroller is so tall that he can hardly see who is behind it. Then, he hears a click on the wheels, and a middle-aged-looking mother emerges from behind.

"Good afternoon," Dr. Liu greets her.

She does not greet him, but says, "Sir," as she stares at him, pausing unexpectedly. She appears to have something in mind, perhaps some non-health issue.

"What can I do for you?" says Dr. Liu, waiting to know the purpose of her coming.

"Sir, I have a problem with my three children," she says.

"What problem do they have?" he asks.

"They don't have any problems," she answers.

"But you have just said they have a problem," says he.

She rolls her eyes over his face, thinks for a moment, and says, "The problem is not with the children. It is with me. It is with you!"

"I am confused," says Dr. Liu. "Did you say your children's problem is with you? And did you say the problem is with me?"

"I am Lucy. You gave me acupuncture treatment about a year and a half ago," she says. "Do you still remember me?"

Oh, do I still remember you? Dr. Liu says to himself. I certainly do! That day, you came with your husband. Your husband was forty-one or forty-two and you were thirty-seven or thirty-eight, I think. You both looked dismayed, dejected, and depressed. You told me that you could not conceive the natural way, so you had tried in-vitro fertilization twice and had failed both times. You were emotionally, physically, and financially involved in both cycles. You wanted a baby badly and when you failed you just could not face the fact. The second failure devastated you even more. You said you were desperate, you were approaching forty and were running out of time, and if you did not have a baby you might never have one. But, as God had arranged it, you came to see me, and so we got to know each other.

I conducted a pulse test for you, and you started your acupuncture treatment immediately. You cooperated with me and came for a course of treatment. I think you came once a day for a period of twenty days. I regulated your hormones, enhanced your energy level, improving your entire system all at the same time. You felt you had become a new person and you left happily. You were all smiles when you said goodbye to me. Yes, it was about eighteen months ago. But I don't know what happened to you afterward.

And here I see your twins sitting side by side on the stroller. Aren't you happy yet? Oh dear, I see another baby moving on the top. So, did you give birth to triplets after my acupuncture treatment?

"I certainly do, Lucy," answers Dr. Liu. "I remember you and your husband wanted a baby badly. You tried in-vitro fertilization twice without success."

"Yes, that's what we did," she says. "It was such a terrible experience for me. I made so many visits to the fertility doctor and received numerous injections throughout each cycle. Both cycles were not only time consuming but also very expensive; each cost us about $30,000. We nearly went broke."

"May I ask, what happened after you left me?" asks Dr. Liu.

"The following month, I finally became pregnant," she says indifferently.

"And you had a live birth, of course," says Dr. Liu.

"Yes, and that is the problem that has brought me here

today," she says, looking displeased.

"If your babies have any problems, they should see a pediatrician instead," says Dr. Liu. "They are too young for acupuncture treatment."

"My babies are perfectly healthy. They don't need to see the pediatrician," Lucy says.

"That's good." Dr. Liu breathes a sigh of relief, still wondering what she has come for.

"Sir, I will be straight to the point," Lucy says in a stern, loud voice that shocks Dr. Liu. "You gave me the twenty treatments and cured my infertility problem, and I appreciate it. But my husband and I only wanted one baby. Having two would be okay for us too. But, sir, why didn't you consult us first? Why on earth did you give us three babies?" She suddenly bursts into tears.

Dr. Liu is not prepared for such a situation, and before he can respond he hears her talking again.

"Three months ago, I gave birth to triplets! Having triplets is just too much for us." She draws a breath and then continues. "We were already broke after the two unsuccessful in-vitro fertilization cycles. We just didn't have the money for three babies. The baby formula, clothes, beddings, bath essentials, everything is so expensive. Besides, the care the babies demand is just unimaginable. The three babies want to be fed at the same time, and sometimes I just don't know which one to feed first. When the first one is being fed, the other two keep crying. I put them to sleep at the same time, but they wake up at different times. One may wake up one hour before the second one, and the second one may wake up forty minutes before the third. They keep me spinning around. Some days, I don't even have the time to eat, and I cannot sleep more than three hours a night, because they keep waking me up. Nursing the triplets is just like working at a conveyer line. It's boring and it never stops. I've been working like a machine, twenty-four hours a day, seven days a week, for three months already. And it gets harder and harder as they get bigger and bigger. You don't know how hard it is! And don't forget my parents have been helping us.

"I have lost twenty-five pounds within three months, which I don't really mind anyway, because, as you know, I was kind of overweight. My husband is also working like a horse. He has to do two jobs to earn enough money to buy baby formula and all the other stuff. A bag of diapers costs $15, a can of formula costs $25, and a tiny baby shirt, $30. These things add up. The triplets eat so much, and they use up the diapers and everything so quickly. For God's sake, sir, why did you give us three children instead of just one, or two at most?"

"Look, Lucy," says Dr. Liu, "I want you to understand that I am just a doctor. I cured your infertility problem. You wanted to be pregnant, and I am happy I succeeded in helping you achieve your goal after your two IVF failures. But you must know your triplets are gifts given to you by God. I am a human. I could not decide how many children you would have. They are God-given gifts; you should appreciate God's gifts. I understand it is a tremendous amount of work for you and your husband now, but when they grow up, you will be proud of them, and you will also be proud of yourself."

Dr. Liu's mentioning of "God-given gifts" seems to have struck a chord in her heart. Her eyes suddenly brighten up, as her body shivers a little. She raises both hands to cover her face. Is she happy? Is she sad? Or is she feeling guilty of having unfairly blamed Dr. Liu? She wipes her tears on her sleeve and says, "Dr. Liu, please forgive me. Please forgive me for my ignorance. I do love my God-given gifts. I am grateful to God. I love my children. I do. I want to thank you again for your great treatment. Without it, my husband and I would still be childless. Thank you! Thank you, indeed!"

Life Regained

May was diagnosed with uterine fibroids, benign tumors on the wall of the uterus. Hoping for a quick cure, she saw one doctor after another, but she experienced more anxiety than positive results. Contrary to her expectations, the more treatments she received, the worse her condition became.

Three years later, she began to suffer from menstrual hemorrhaging, or profuse bleeding from the womb. Her abnormally heavy and prolonged menstrual bleeding continued for more than two years, despite the many visits she had made to two gynecologists, among other doctors. Every person has so much blood in the body. If you bleed too much for too long, your body will eventually reach the point where it can no longer function, and death will be awaiting you.

Then came the day when May found her deteriorating condition severely affecting her life and work. She felt weak and dizzy at home and in the office. May knew she was racing against time. In desperation, she sought advice from friends and bloggers.

Two bloggers had advised her to see specialists of traditional Chinese medicine (TCM), and she did. She tried three of them. One herbal specialist and one acupuncturist, but neither was able to improve her condition. Her last alternative medical practitioner combined herbal medicine and acupuncture in her treatment, which seemed to have improved her condition a little in the beginning, but it still did not work effectively. Her instinct told her that even the third one could not cure her illness.

Though devastated, May refused to give up. She continued to look for the right doctor for herself, but unfortunately, before she found effective help, on December 24, while driving on the road after her treatment from the third alternative medical practitioner, she fainted behind the wheel.

"I thought I was dying," May recalled afterward. "Everyone thought I was dying. I was so weak and so sick. I had lost all my strength when I passed out. Then, someone fed me a cup of cold water, and I regained consciousness. As if pre-arranged by God, this was a turning point in my life."

Below is May's own narration of the rest of her story.

"After I regained consciousness that day, I decided not to go back to my alternative medical practitioner, but I didn't have another doctor to see. Yet, I could not sit idly waiting for death to come.

"Patience is golden, and indeed persistence prevails. I looked through the ads in one of the health magazines, and I happened to find Dr. Liu. I called him immediately. Don't forget it was Christmastime. To be more accurate, it was Christmas Eve. I wouldn't be surprised if he asked me to wait until after Christmas for treatment.

"To my surprise, Dr. Liu was so friendly and so kind, saying he could see me immediately. I had been losing so much blood for such a long time and had just passed out, and he knew any further delay could cost my life. He asked me to go to his clinic at once, and so I did. You don't know how grateful I was and how much I appreciated his timely treatment!

"He gave me a pulse test, looked at my tongue and lips. Then, he told me everything about my illness, which I knew well. What he told me just confirmed that he was such a knowledgeable doctor who diagnosed every one of my symptoms so accurately. He said my blood pressure was extremely low, and it was. He said I was extremely weak, and I was. He said I felt dizzy all the time, and I did. That his diagnosis was accurate was not important to me anymore.

What I needed most was treatment, and indeed he gave me my first treatment as soon as my diagnosis was completed.

"My feeling after Dr. Liu's first treatment differed from that I had from all the other alternative medical practitioners. At once I felt hope. I knew something positive inside me was happening, and it was happening somewhere deep down at the root level. The moment I got up from the acupuncture bed, I felt I was going to be a different person in due time.

"Dr. Liu told me to come every day, stressing that I must come so that the treatment efficacy could be maintained at its best. I didn't really need his reminder. I was so sick and I had already placed full confidence in this knowledgeable, experienced, and caring doctor.

"I returned to Dr. Liu's clinic on Christmas Day. He was waiting for me when I arrived. A doctor in Toronto working for his patients on Christmas Day! I cannot hold back my tears even today when I think of this. Thus, I had my second treatment; then, the third; and then, the fourth... My once uncontrollable bleeding slowed down and soon it stopped. I felt stronger and stronger.

"After Dr. Liu stopped my bleeding, he began to deal with my uterine fibroids, the real cause of my long years of bleeding. Honestly, without experiencing the positive results, I was still uncertain, or anxious rather, if the fibroids could be controlled by acupuncture. After all, Dr. Liu was only using those tiny needles, but then I thought, if the tiny needles could stop my bleeding, why couldn't they perform magically on the tumors as well? Anyway, I didn't need any physics theory to explain any of this, and I did not really trust the modern theory and treatment that had not worked for me in the first place. All I wanted was a cure for my chronic disease, for which I kept praying to God. But I dared not show my anxiety or share it with the doctor, lest I hurt his feelings.

"After a month of acupuncture treatment, I went back to my conventional gynecologist, who prescribed another hysteroscopy for me. Three days later, the specialist, in disbelief, told me that the lab reports showed that my largest 7 cm fibroid had shrunk to less than 1 cm, and the smaller ones had all disappeared. What a miracle it was! What medical theory, physics theory, or chemistry theory could clearly explain what the tiny needles were doing inside my body and how this could have ever happened?

"But does it matter to a patient? In my case, I had regained my good health and subsequently my life. After becoming a healthy person again, I continued to work as a holistic nutritionist and an environmental lifestyle counselor. Looking back, I realize that I not only had survived in life but have thrived in my business. With no exaggeration, I owe today's good health and happy life to Dr. Liu. And Dr. Liu alone!"

Miracle Acupuncturist

It all started with the sudden change on her daughter's tongue. One day, her 27-year-old daughter discovered a 2 cm wide black stripe running from the back of her tongue to the apex. It became a cause of worry for Mrs. Watson, who had studied acupuncture herself. She knew that something must have gone wrong in her daughter's immune system. It could be related to oral lichen planus, an incurable chronic condition that affects the mucous membranes inside the mouth. She believed that conventional doctors would hesitate to prescribe medications or other treatment for such a condition. Therefore, she opted for alternative medicine, for which she had to pay out of her own pocket.

Mrs. Watson took her daughter to an experienced practitioner of traditional Chinese medicine in Toronto who used be a royal physician for Chiang Kai-shek of Taiwan. The TCM practitioner prescribed herbal medications for the patient for a week but failed to improve her condition and therefore asked her to seek treatment from other medical professionals. The following day, Mrs. Watson found another renowned herbal practitioner, who prescribed a total of 103 packages of herbs for her daughter, but he also failed to improve her condition. "Do you want to see Dr. Liu upstairs instead?" he finally asked Mrs. Watson and her daughter. "He is next to none in acupuncture. If he is not the best, then no one is."

Mrs. Watson said yes and they went upstairs to see Dr. Liu. Ironically, Mrs. Watson, who had studied acupuncture, had known Dr. Liu prior to her visit, but she just had never thought that acupuncture could cure diseases.

Dr. Liu immediately gave her daughter a pulse test, discovering that she had a condition that the other two TCM practitioners had failed to diagnose accurately. In TCM terms, she had a rare double condition of "heat" and "cold" caused by "dampness," originating from her weak spleen. If a practitioner prescribed medicine to control her "heat" condition only, it would cause her other condition to deteriorate, and vice versa. That was the reason why the previous practitioners had failed to cure her. He said that the patient needed "nourishment" treatment instead.

Dr. Liu gave the patient fifteen acupuncture treatments, once daily. This course of treatment cured it thoroughly. Mrs. Watson was impressed by Dr. Liu's miraculous treatment.

Unfortunately, Mrs. Watson fell ill herself the following month. She was diagnosed with pneumonia, coughing nonstop. She received treatment from conventional doctors and practitioners of alternative medicine as well. She was sent to the hospital twice during her 120 days of treatment.

In the beginning, she ran a low fever in the afternoon, which would then disappear, but when she slept at night, she would wet her pillow by 6:00 a.m. After her family doctor failed to control the condition with ten days of medications, her condition deteriorated so rapidly that he had to send her to the hospital for emergency treatment. By then, her lungs had swollen so badly that collecting a sample from her lungs was impossible. Finally, the doctor in the hospital just gave her intravenous injections without completing the routine tests. Fortunately, he managed to bring her condition under control within a day.

Mrs. Watson was then discharged from the hospital and asked to take two weeks of medications at home, but her illness was far from being cured. Not long after she finished her medications, her bad cough not only came back, but it deteriorated until she could hardly breathe, and so she was taken by ambulance to the hospital again, this time to the Lesley hospital where she was quarantined. She was suspected of having tuberculosis. Fortunately, it turned out to be a false alarm. After three days of intensive treatment, she was released from quarantining and went home.

After three months of treatment, her lung trouble was finally cured. Nonetheless, the powerful medications including the antibiotics and the injections had caused many side effects and sequelae. She was now suffering from insomnia and was allergic to bread, flowers, and plants; and the list of her sequelae goes on. To add pain to misery, two weeks later, she was diagnosed with kidney infection, for which she received treatment from the conventional doctors again.

When her kidney infection was cured, her right arm became numb and painful. Believing she had taken too much powerful "chemical" medicine, she sought treatment from a TCM practitioner instead, who prescribed three packages of herbal medications for her. After she took them, she could not even raise her arm at all. Only then did she think of Dr. Liu again. How she regretted that she had not gone to see him earlier!

Dr. Liu gave her one acupuncture treatment on the day she saw him, and she was able to raise her arm! Then, he gave her four more treatments, and she was thoroughly cured. How miraculous it was!

On her way home from her last visit to Dr. Liu, Mrs. Watson stopped at T&T to buy some groceries. Then, when she was turning left on Steeles Avenue East at Warden, out of nowhere came a flying van that smashed her car into a hydro post. Everyone said she was lucky to be alive. Her car was ruined but she emerged from the wreck without visible injuries. She was not sure if she was injured at all when the ambulance arrived, but the paramedics took her to the hospital anyway.

The emergency doctor glanced at her and then prescribed pain relievers for her after she complained about chest pain. Believing she had not been injured, as he could not find a single scratch or a drop of blood on her, he discharged her without even taking an X-ray of her painful chest.

After Mrs. Watson went home, her chest pain deteriorated rapidly, and the painkillers could hardly ease it. Unable to eat, sit, and sleep, she groaned in agony until the next morning. She skipped breakfast and went to see her family doctor without an appointment, arriving there before his clinic opened. Her sympathetic family doctor immediately prescribed an X-ray examination for her, which revealed an unmistakable broken sternum.

The family doctor told her she should contact the insurance company that would, besides paying for the repairs or replacement of her car, arrange free treatment for her and pay her for her loss of work due to her injury. Mrs. Watson thought that the free treatment would usually be physiotherapy that might not be the most effective and that such arrangements and relevant approval from the insurance company would take too long. This time, she did not want to put her health in jeopardy, so she went to see Dr. Liu directly.

She told him about the traffic accident and the acute pain she was suffering in the breastbone area. After examining her condition, Dr. Liu gave her acupuncture treatment immediately, which relieved her pain on the same day.

After twenty treatments, her pain disappeared completely. She felt as energetic and as healthy as before. The following day, she went back to her family doctor on Steeles Avenue, who prescribed another X-ray examination for her. When the reports came, he called her back to his office and they went over the details together. The break in her breastbone, which would usually take three to six months to heal, was nowhere to be found. He asked her what had happened. She told him about the acupuncture treatment she had received from Dr. Liu.

"It's a miracle," said the family doctor in disbelief.

When Mrs. Watson's friends heard about her recovery from the injury caused by the terrible traffic accident, they all called to congratulate her upon her lucky survival and rapid recovery.

"I truly believed in Dr. Liu, that is why I recovered faster," she told her friends.

Her overjoyed Indian friend sent her a box of biscuits with a large package of tea inside. When Mrs. Watson returned home, she opened the box, brewed the tea, and then began to enjoy the delicious biscuits that went perfectly well with the strong, fragrant tea. How tasty the biscuits were and how refreshing the tea was! What a happy moment she had!

But to her panic, within ten minutes she had a sudden onset of diarrhea, followed by vomiting. She tried to sit back after the first vomit, but moments later she burst out vomiting again. Soon it became uncontrollable. She kept vomiting every ten seconds or so. Before long, she was throwing up green vomit.

She became scared now, not knowing what had happened to her and what to do. She could not make it to the washroom several times, so her living room did not look or smell very pleasant now. *If I continue vomiting like this*, she thought, *I'll die of suffocation or a heart attack.*

Undeniably, it was an emergency. She thought of calling the ambulance for assistance, but she was afraid of going to the hospital again. Then, she thought of seeing Dr. Liu, but how could she drive to his clinic since she would vomit every ten or fifteen seconds? Finally, she plucked up her courage and called Dr. Liu, asking if he could come to see her in her home. She told him that she was too sick to go to his clinic. On hearing her description of her illness, Dr. Liu said, "Seeing you at your home is not a problem, but before I make my trip, I want you to try one acupuncture point. If it stops your vomiting, I don't need to go. If it doesn't, I will go and see you."

Then, Dr. Liu told her to locate an acupoint on her arm, somewhere between her wrist and the elbow and press it with her finger. Mrs. Watson did it as instructed. To her disbelief, as soon as she pressed it, her vomiting stopped!

"What a miracle!" she said in a low, feeble voice. "*Fing-*

upuncture?" Her phone was still connected with Dr. Liu, but he could not hear her words.

Mrs. Watson was just as shocked by the mysterious stopping of her vomiting as she was by its sudden onset. Finding herself immersed in turbulent emotions, she burst out crying, startling Dr. Liu who was still waiting for the results of her *Fing-upuncture*.

"You are a great miracle acupuncturist indeed!" she cried chokingly. "You have cured my vomiting without even seeing me!"

Bedtime Story for a 4-Month-Old

Kate Felreal's life changed after her baby was born four months ago. Every cell in her body was soaked in the joy and happiness of motherhood. At times, she spoke like a lunatic, especially when mother and child were alone at home. This evening she became even more talkative with her 4-month-old son.

"My angel, my darling, my dearest, you bring me such joy and happiness every day, every moment. I am so grateful to you! As you know, your father has gone on a business trip to Ottawa and won't be home tonight, so we can talk as much as we want to, and you can stay up as late as you like.

"Great, my angel. You are smiling! For our bedtime story tonight, I want to tell you one that is not from a library book. It's a real story about you, me, and your father. Maybe you will not remember it, but I hope you will. I hope it will stay in your memory. Throughout the past four months I kept wondering if I should wait until you are older—perhaps when you go to kindergarten or elementary school or high school or when you have grown up or when you have become a father yourself. But then I thought, the older you are, the better you will understand the story, and then the more awkward I may feel when I tell you the story. So, I have decided to tell you the story now.

"Now here you go.

"Your father and I got married five years ago. We had a great wedding attended by over 100 friends, relatives, and colleagues. Like many other married couples, we wanted to have a child. Our obstetrician joked that raising a child is a 24-year contract. We know raising a child in our city is an expensive investment and a long-term commitment, but without a child, we would not consider our marriage a complete success. Without a child, I could not be called a mother, and our family could not be a real, happy one.

"We planned to have a child one year after our marriage, but we did not have one. We tried one more year and failed another year. The more we tried, the more eager we were and the more badly we wanted one. Yet, the more anxious we were, the more distressed we became. We reached the point of desperation when we failed to have a child even in the third year. Did it mean we could be a childless couple forever? I cried to myself many times, jealous of other wives who had given birth to babies without complications. How happy they were, I imagined!

"Though feeling rather embarrassed, your father and I went to see a fertility doctor, called a reproductive endocrinologist. Then, we went through all kinds of tests. At the age of thirty-seven, I was informed that we had a fertility problem and that I could not conceive the natural way. The fertility doctor told us we could only go for in-vitro fertilization, or IVF. It was still good news for me, but my excitement was chilled immediately when he told us that the rate of live birth at my age was not very high. It sounded like a very risky adventure. Then, he went on with more details. Apparently, it was a long and difficult procedure, but for a child, I would embrace any challenges and endure any hardships.

"My darling, the doctor warned us that in my age group, on average, only one in every four embryos implanted resulted in a live birth. That means three out of four would fail. In other words, couples might have to try more than one round of embryo implantation. The average was three rounds, he said. The estimated cost per cycle, including treatments and medications, was $20,000, so three rounds would cost about $60,000. That did not include the loss of pay due to loss of work, but the number one issue was the agonizing anxiety that money could not prevent.

"We still wanted to try, but we did not want to be an average couple that would take three cycles to succeed. We wanted to succeed in the first trial. We wanted to be parents within the shortest time possible. Brushing aside all concerns and worries, we began to find ways to avoid complications.

"My dearest, you frown at me. You want to know what we did, don't you?

"I turned on my computer and googled if acupuncture could increase the success rate of in-vitro fertilization. I quickly discovered that several fertility clinics affiliated with reputed American universities, in fact, used acupuncture in the in-vitro fertilization process. I then checked the cost of acupuncture. Compared with that of the IVF procedure, it was only a small fraction.

"I was more than happy to go for acupuncture to improve our chance of IVF success. Without delay, I started looking for a good acupuncturist in our city. My searching soon led me to Dr. Liu, an internationally well-known acupuncturist who had many success stories posted online. I contacted him and made an appointment with him for an in-person consultation.

"My angel, you are yawning. I know you want to sleep. I will cut the story short then.

"Indeed, Dr. Liu was worthy of his name. He had, without medications, miraculously cured many patients, including husbands and wives with fertility problems. I was in good hands. The year before my IVF trial, Dr. Liu gave me five acupuncture treatments that regulated my hormones, which was crucial in the IVF procedure. He not only enhanced my energy level but also reduced my anxiety and improved my quality of sleep.

"When my IVF procedure started the following year, I started seeing him again, receiving another ten acupuncture treatments. Again, he regulated my entire system by reducing my anxiety and improving my sleep. As a result, I felt great throughout the long and difficult procedure that involved numerous visits to the fertility doctor and daily injections that kind of scared me in the end. Despite all the challenges, everything ended well.

"When the fertility doctor was implanting the fertilized eggs, he told me that my uterus was in perfect shape with the healthiest lining. I have little medical knowledge, but I believe the acupuncture had increased the blood flow to the uterus and subsequently improved its overall health. My guessing is not important anyway. What matters to me, my angel, my darling, my dearest, is that you were born on June 29 of this year. Without Dr. Liu's acupuncture treatment, I am not sure if I could have been pregnant at all and if you could have ever come to this world. I am forever grateful to Dr. Liu for his help.

"I will see him again soon when your father and I decide to start a new IVF procedure to have a brother or sister for you. I want you and your brother or sister to remember Dr. Liu's important contribution to our family's happy life when you grow up.

"I see you smiling, sweet angel. You understand me! Thank you! Night-night!"

Birthday-ache

Hagen Carleton unlocked the front door, pushed it open, and said, "Hi, Honey!" Out came his wife, Carol, who dropped a kiss on his lips as she threw a bear hug around him in the foyer. He conveniently lifted her off her feet and swung her around in a circle. That was something the loving couple enjoyed doing when Hagen came home from work every day. He then hung his coat, removed his shoes, and headed toward the living room.

No sooner had he taken his first step than his wife and their three children shouted in chorus, "Happy birthday!" Then, they started singing the birthday song to him.

"Thank you!" Hagen smiled, realizing he had forgotten his own birthday.

The children loved cakes, so they would have the cake before dinner. He blew out the candle, cut the cake, and gave each child a quarter. He and Carol shared the rest. Everyone was all smiles—the cake on everybody's birthday always made everyone smile.

"Ouch!" Hagen suddenly shouted, surprising everyone.

"What happened, Daddy?" asked Mike, the eldest child. His whole family was waiting for an answer.

"My toe, it suddenly hurt," he groaned. "It has been bothering me for some time, but it never hurt so much. But never mind. It'll be gone in a few minutes. Just go on enjoying your cake."

He was right. The pain disappeared within five minutes, but so did the beaming smiles on the children's faces.

"Isn't it annoying," Hagen said to himself. "Why did it have to happen at this moment?"

Hagen's left long toe had been irritating him since his last birthday. Last winter, it felt like it had been frostbitten, but there was no chance it could have been exposed to the freezing weather, for he was always wearing warm socks and boots and never felt cold. He suspected that the irritation could have more likely been caused by the rubbing of the boot, but his boots were not new. In fact, he had worn them for three winters, and they had never caused any discomfort.

Hagen removed the sock and took a close look at the aching toe. He found it kind of reddish, but there was no visible swelling or infection. Equally annoying was that he had a similar attack in his office when they were celebrating their manager's birthday the previous Monday. On both occasions it just ruined the happy atmosphere. Hagen decided to do something about it.

The following afternoon, he was seeing his family doctor. The doctor, who had been practicing medicine for over thirty years, examined his toe carefully but could not find anything wrong with it.

"It appears to be a normal toe, and there's no sign of frostbite," he said. He could not tell Hagen the name of his condition, because Hagen did not seem to have one. As such, the doctor did not even prescribe any medications or other treatment for him.

Hagen walked out of the clinic with mixed feelings: having no trouble was better than having a definite condition, but he was worried it might attack him again.

Indeed, it did! On Carol's birthday three months later, at about the same time, just after they had sung the birthday song and cut the cake, the toe attacked him again. He was in too much pain to refrain from uttering, "Ouch!"

Hagen was sure there must be something wrong with his toe. Otherwise, how could it hurt so badly? Why didn't the other toes hurt anyway? He requested the family doctor's permission to see a rheumatologist and he got it.

To his disappointment, the rheumatologist was not much better than his family doctor. He could not match the pain on his toe with any condition described in the textbooks. The rheumatologist had completed a four-year undergraduate degree, four years of medical school and five years of rheumatology studies, plus twenty-some years of clinical experience. Hagen knew he was a competent specialist.

"Your toe's skin looks perfectly healthy. There is no swelling and no infection. I don't see anything abnormal there," he told Hagen. "You know, the human body is a funny system. Sometimes something out of the ordinary just happens and we just don't have an answer for it."

"Do you want to prescribe some medications for me, just in case?" asked Hagen.

"I don't see the need for it. Since there is no condition, medications will not help," said the rheumatologist.

Hagen left in dejection. The fact was he had suffered three attacks already, but neither doctor could identify his condition.

"But you can't blame the doctors either," he said to himself. "When I went to see them, I really had no pain or discomfort."

Then came Christmas, which happened to be Mike's birthday. It was always the most important day for the family. The family tradition was to eat the birthday cake before dinner, followed by the annual celebration of Christmas. The cake was always the first item to be placed on the dining table before Christmas dishes were served.

Mike's parents and siblings sang the birthday song, then he cut the cake, and everyone started eating their delicious slice, but out of the blue, Hagen was seizing his left foot and clenching his teeth again. This time he uttered, "Oh my!" instead. But everybody knew what was happening again.

Hagen really wanted to curse his toe, but it was a double celebration, the most important day for the family, so he just hopped out of the dining room and threw himself onto the sofa in the family room instead. He did not want to spoil the happy occasion, but he had already done so anyway. Sitting on the sofa, he realized that all the attacks had occurred on a birthday, and suddenly he became afraid of birthdays. "Why?" he wondered.

As a precaution, he excused himself from every one of his colleagues' upcoming birthday celebrations. There were fifteen people working in his department, but he would rather not show up at the singing of the birthday song and the cutting of the cake. "I may not suffer a toe attack at every colleague's birthday celebration, but even one or two would be too many," he thought. His strategy seemed to work, and his toe did not attack him again in the office, but Hagen just could not avoid all happy celebrations.

On his mother's sixtieth birthday, which overlapped her fortieth anniversary, his whole family was invited to the sumptuous celebration. By now you would not be surprised if Hagen got into trouble with his toe again after the large beautiful cake was cut.

It just happened again! This time it was more painful than ever before. He put pressure on the base of his toe with both hands, hoping to suppress the pain. Before long, his head and face were covered with sweat. Carol, who was sitting next to him, knew what was happening. She held his hand and led him away to a more private place—the laundry room.

"This Goddamn toe," he cursed under his breath. "I wish I could just chop it off!" He felt really humiliated, so he decided to do something one way or another. He suspected it might be a neurological condition. The next morning, he made an appointment with a neurologist for the following Friday. The neurologist checked everything carefully, and like the previous doctors, he said he could not identify the condition.

"How could it be? Why could none of the doctors find the cause of my unbearable pain? What trouble could it really be?"

Hagen complained to the neurologist.

"I apologize for my inability to identify it," said the neurologist.

"Oh God!" Hagen said. "I have never heard of anyone having an illness that so many doctors cannot name. I do know that our Canadian-trained doctors have a name for every single disease they treat. I always thought the doctors had a longer list of disease names than the vocabulary most Canadians use in their daily life. But why not a name for my condition?!" Hagen sounded impatient and impolite.

"I feel bad about it too," said the neurologist.

Hagen did not know what to do with his toe anymore. Though he had also thought of seeing a dermatologist or a massage therapist, he had no confidence in them, so he just gave up.

All the doctors he had seen only told him that it was not gout, but none of them knew what it was, and none of them could treat his condition. As a result, none of them ever prescribed any medications for him.

"Oh gosh," sighed Hagen. "If you do not even have a name for the condition, that means you don't even know what it is. If you don't know what it is, how could you ever cure it?" Finally, he decided not to see any more doctors, and he would stay far away from all parties, especially birthday parties. Meanwhile, he had bought a large package of earplugs, which he could use on anybody's birthday at home and in the office. He had also bought plenty of Tylenol and kept it within reach, just in case.

Most mysteriously, the toe-ache hurt him like a toothache. It came and went unpredictably. Later, it even struck him on neighbors' and strangers' birthdays, whenever he heard the singing of the birthday song. Despite all his precautions, these attacks still occurred, usually twice a month, during a period of over ten years.

On his second son's most recent birthday, it not only hurt unbearably (though he was sitting on the back porch), but it caused numbness in his entire left leg, which fortunately disappeared the next day. Then, on his daughter's birthday in the same year, though he hid himself in the bedroom upstairs, the moment he heard the family singing the birthday song, he had the most severe attack ever. He felt as if his toe was on fire and being pounded by a hammer at the same time. The acute pain went from his toe right through his spine. He kept kicking his foot to ease it. When that failed, he tried to squeeze the calf to numb the nerves connected with it, but it did not work. The unendurable pain still had to take its own course. It even lasted until the small hours of the next morning. Undeniably his condition was deteriorating rapidly. Each attack was more severe and lasted longer than the previous.

"No. I can't let this happen like this forever!" His mind made up, he started looking for alternative treatment instead.

As the story has it, Hagen found Dr. Wan Cheng Liu, a world-renowned acupuncturist in Regina. He saw him the following day.

Dr. Liu gave him a pulse test and found the cause of his aching toe.

"Your aching toe looks like a mystery, but it is not," Dr. Liu told Hagen. "Actually, you have more than just a sore toe. You have several other problems: sore shoulders, congestion around the heart area, high blood pressure, and lack of energy. Your other doctors knew about them, but they did not treat these conditions for you. I don't have an official name for your aching toe either, but traditional Chinese medicine does not care as much about accurate disease names and symptoms of every patient. Personally, I treat my patients holistically, based on my clinical experience. My priority is curing your illness, whether I have an accurate name for the disease or not. You want me to treat your toe, and I will treat it for you, along with your other health problems. If I just treat your toe, you won't have the best treatment results."

"Wow, you know everything about my body," Hagen said.

"How long will my acupuncture treatment last?"

"You will need a period of fifteen treatments, one treatment per day," said Dr. Liu, "After that, we will see if you need more." Hagen accepted his advice.

"Since the toe is what you have come to treat, I will treat it as a priority on the first day, but as I have just said, you can't just treat the toe, because it wouldn't work that way. I need to treat your entire system, including the congestion of your chest, your sore shoulders and high blood pressure."

Hagen's first treatment started immediately after his diagnostic test. Like many other patients, he looked a little nervous in the beginning, but after the needles were flicked into his acupoints, he soon fell asleep. When he woke up, he felt much better holistically, and the pain and numbness on the toe had improved. After he completed his fifteen treatments, his ailments were all cured.

"Dr. Liu, may I ask exactly how you cured my sore toe?" he asked.

"Well, your toe is at the end of your foot where blood may not always flow smoothly, especially when you have a blockage. In your case, once the blockage was cleared and once your *qi* and blood circulated smoothly through the system, the sore naturally disappeared. In Chinese medicine, we say, 'Blockage means pain; no blockage, no pain.' I hope I have answered your question."

"Thank you! You have taught me such a valuable lesson on Chinese medicine," said Hagen. "But Dr. Liu, why did all my attacks happen on birthdays?"

"They could be coincidental," said Dr. Liu. "But if all of them or most of them really occurred on birthdays, then they could have been triggered by your anxiety or other emotional factors. For example, if you were worried about something or scared of something, or if you felt nervous and sweated or shivered, it could have affected the flow of your *qi* and blood and triggered the attacks."

"That makes sense, Dr. Liu," said Hagen. "In fact, whenever I heard the birthday song, I really felt nervous and started sweating. I don't know why."

"There will be no more toe attacks. Just relax and enjoy any birth celebrations you can attend," said Dr. Liu.

Hagen smiled, still in disbelief that Dr. Liu had, in fifteen days, cured his 10-year-old toe-ache after other conventional doctors had failed. To express his heartfelt gratitude to him for his unbelievable treatment, Hagen wrote a letter in praise of his profound knowledge and great expertise. He sent it to the local newspaper, hoping to share his treatment story with other patients who had similar conditions so that they would know where to seek treatment without delay.

COVID-19 Patients

It was a Sunday afternoon before the March 2020 lockdown. Dr. Liu was resting in his armchair in his private room in the clinic before his next appointment. Hardly had he closed his eyes for a brief nap when he heard his phone ringing. He picked it up after the second ring and said hello. Then he heard a lady's voice.

"Can I speak to Dr. Liu, please?" she said.

"Speaking," said Dr. Liu. Then, there was silence. "What can I do for you?" he continued.

"It's Christina, Dr. Liu," she finally said. "I am sick. I am embarrassed to ask if I could come and see you."

"What trouble do you have?" asked Dr. Liu.

"I have caught the COVID-19 virus. Can acupuncture cure it?" she said.

"It depends on how sick you are. If you are in the early stage, yes. I should be able to cure it, but if it has got deep into your lungs, it may be more difficult," said Dr. Liu.

"I don't know if I am in the beginning stage or not, but I am sure it hasn't got deep into my lungs yet," she said.

"Where did you get it?" asked Dr. Liu.

"I am a nurse working in the General Hospital. I got it at work," she said.

"A nurse working in the General Hospital," Dr. Liu repeated.

"I look after COVID-19 patients every day," she said. "Several nurses and doctors in my department also have been infected with the virus. We all caught it this week."

"I see. Come over to my clinic as soon as you can, and I will help you," said Dr. Liu. "I will give you acupuncture treatment and prescribe some Chinese herbal medications for you, if necessary."

"But it is very contagious," said Christina. "If I come to your clinic, you may catch it too. It could be deadly."

"We are both medical workers. You risk your life saving patients' lives. When you come, you are my patient. Saving my patients' lives is my job. If I have to get it, I shall get it. If one of us has to die, I shall go first."

Christina was deeply touched, knowing there was a stranger in this world who cared more about her life than his own. She had witnessed firsthand how some doctors stopped working and how some nurses resigned from their jobs just to stay away from the coronavirus. She had also seen screaming COVID-19 patients in the intensive care unit struggling with breathing and fighting for their lives. The horrific gasps of dying patients before breathing their last haunted her, especially after she had been infected with the same virus.

She knew that it could happen to anyone, often within a matter of days and unexpectedly. On one busy day, she had personally seen three patients who came to the overcrowded hospital for emergency treatment but were just told to go back home to "rest and monitor the condition." They were asked to "come back if the condition deteriorates," but they never came back. Within the same week the coronavirus took all their lives. Sadder still, their relatives and friends could not even attend their funerals. Their deaths were just cruel in every aspect.

Christina was not surprised when she tested COVID-19 positive. She knew she would be infected sooner or later. She just hoped that she could recover from the infection because her family needed her and the patients in the hospital needed her care badly. Her life depended upon the doctor she had not yet seen and the treatment she was yet to receive.

It was 4:00 p.m. when she arrived at Dr. Liu's clinic. She

was even more shocked when she met him. Dr. Liu appeared to be in his seventies, obviously belonging to the most fragile age groups that should not be exposed to the coronavirus. He should at least stay away from COVID-19 patients. Yet, he feared no death and was even willing to die for her if death had to occur. Tears streamed down her face as she stood still in Dr. Liu's clinic, thinking about the previous doctor she had called, whose assistant only took her phone number and said that he would call her back within two business days. She knew a wait of two business days without treatment or medications could cost her life.

Dr. Liu gave her a pulse test, followed by acupuncture treatment. Unlike in 2003, when he treated a dying SARS patient without wearing a mask himself and was infected with the virus on the patient's first day of treatment (he did not have a mask in the clinic then), he wore a mask this time. It was not an N-95, but still better than none.

"It's good you came early," he told Christina. "You will be fine. You should recover within four or five days." After the treatment, he prescribed for her two types of cold-relieving herbal medications and instructed her on how to use them at home. She did as instructed, and her condition started to improve the next morning. She returned for her second treatment and continued to take her herbal medications. On the third day she knew she was free of lung infection. On the fifth day, she had recovered—she had no more fever, headache, coughing, painful muscles, or other COVID-19 symptoms. She was a healthy, energetic person again.

"I seem to have recovered from my COVID infection," Christina told Dr. Liu on the phone. "I feel really great now."

"Good!" said Dr. Liu.

"Thank you so much, Dr. Liu! I owe my rapid recovery to you. I don't know what might have happened to me without your effective treatment," she said. "You risked your life to save mine."

"I am glad you have recovered," said Dr. Liu.

"Do I need to come for more treatment?" she asked.

"No," said Dr. Liu. "You are a nurse and since you think you have recovered, you have. You don't need to come again, but do call me if anything unexpectedly happens to you within the next few days, which is very unlikely."

Two weeks later, again, at about 1:00 pm, Dr. Liu heard his phone ringing when he had just finished his lunch.

"I am sorry, Dr. Liu. It's Christina again."

"Never mind," said Dr. Liu. "What can I do for you?"

"My husband and my daughter have also caught the Covid-19 virus," she said. "They have a headache, a runny nose, and a sore throat. Could they come and see you?"

"They don't need to come to see me yet," said Dr. Liu. "Come to my clinic and get the herbal medications for them. Try two days and see what happens. If they don't get better, call me and I will see them."

Immediately, Christina rushed back to Dr. Liu's clinic to buy the medications for them. Her husband and daughter took them as instructed. Amazingly, the inexpensive herbal medications, usually used to relieve common colds, were very effective for COVID-19 patients. The following day, their condition improved. Three days later, they both recovered. It was such a relief for Christina.

She truly felt that she was a lucky one, compared with some of her colleagues who were infected in the same week but had a much tougher fight, which even resulted in one death, as reported on April 7. Saddened by the news of her colleague's death, Christina shuddered, knowing it could have happened to her and her family had they not sought treatment from Dr. Liu.

What impressed her most was that Dr. Liu had fearlessly risked his life to save hers and other patients', and that though he was in his seventies, he still worked tirelessly for his patients, seven days a week, treating every patient equally, regardless of their gender, age, appearance, culture, race, and occupation—and regardless of their illness!

"What an experience we have been through!" Christina said to her family. "It's all about the knowledge and expertise of your doctor. Something that seems very easy for one may be a matter of life and death for another. We are among the luckiest ones of the Covid-19 patients."

Alternative to Surgery

Lucia Shapro had just changed into her blue hospital gown and was now waiting for the nurse to take her to the operating room. Suddenly, she burst into tears, sobbing uncontrollably. The nurse, who had seen patients crying, came over to comfort her. In most cases, patients cried because they were sad or scared of the surgeon, scalpel, or blood. Some had even fainted before the surgery took place.

Lucia, however, feared none of those. She had her own problems, which she hated to tell anyone. She was the only secretary in the School of Business at the local community college. She was an indispensable worker in the office who sent out daily emails and other documents to all the faculty and staff members and the hundreds of students.

She had two children aged five and seven who had been depending upon her. She had to cook for them, clean up the table, wash up the dishes, help them with their baths, and do the laundry. She also had to drive them to school and do grocery shopping. The list is goes on, and these errands all required the use of her hands.

She knew that the moment her surgery started, she would not be able to use her hands anymore. She would not even be able to hold a glass of water or lift a plate of food. Even using a fork and knife or just inserting a straw into a juice box would be impossible for her. She would soon become a new-born baby who had to depend on others for everything.

In the past two weeks, to improve her survival skills, Lucia had even secretly tried to train herself to eat without her hands.

She had practiced holding a knife and fork using her right foot. First, she tried to hold a knife between the big toe and the long toe, which was not that difficult. Then, she tried to use the fork to send food into her mouth. That was the hardest part, for she had to bend hard to bring her mouth close to her foot, and moving the food from the plate to her mouth without spilling was just a formidable challenge. Once, her foot pushed the plate with too much force, sending it straight to the floor. Another time, she hurt her mouth with her fork, causing it to bleed throughout the meal.

It was from an armless young man on the internet that Lucia got the idea of learning to feed herself with her foot, but it was not a skill one could learn without sufficient practice. Then, taking advantage of her arms, she tried to learn to hold a long, large wooden spoon with her right elbow. As it turned out, using her elbow was easier than using her foot, but accurately picking up food was still no easy job. She felt proud of the additional skills she had learned, albeit imperfectly. She thought that they could be useful after the surgery in one way or another. Her own survival, however, was never her primary concern.

What worried her the most was her children at home, who had been depending on her since birth. At this moment, she had come to realize that it was her hands that they had been depending upon. It was her hands that had been helping the children and doing everything back home. But soon she would have surgery on both hands, and then her children would be left "without a mother" and, consequentially, without the essential care they needed. The more she thought about her hands, the more haunted she felt for her children's survival. She deeply regretted that she had not made sufficient arrangements for them before coming to the hospital. It was just agonizing.

"Is there anything we can do for you?" asked the nurse.

Lucia shook her head and went on sobbing.

"Are you scared of your surgery?" the nurse asked.

Lucia again shook her head and went on crying.

"Do you faint at blood?" asked the nurse kindly.

Lucia shook her head again but just would not stop crying.

There was no sign she would be emotionally ready for surgery within the next few minutes. With such sobbing and body movements, it would even be difficult for the anesthetist to do his job, and without anesthetization, surgery was impossible. In any case, a patient in such an emotional state was not fit for surgery. Finally, the hospital decided to reschedule her surgery and asked her to go home. The tearful Lucia left the surgery transition room in dejection. Her hands and arms were still as numb and painful as they had been when she arrived.

Lucia only knew surgery was not her best option, but she did not know what other options she had. When she went home, she called the Chair of the college where she worked, still sobbing, telling him she had returned home without having surgery. She told him all the problems her surgery would cause, many of which were unsurmountable. The Chair usually did not want to get involved in his employees' personal issues, but in Lucia's case, he felt he had to help her.

"Lucia, I don't intend to recommend or suggest any option to you, but I'll just tell you about the same problem two other employees in our college had before. Andrea Anderson in the School of English and Communications had her surgery last May, and she came back to work in September. I hear her recovery took just three or four months."

"Did she have trouble with one hand or two?" asked Lucia.

"One. But Paula Pureshire in the Marketing Department had surgery on both hands. She still has some pain now."

"When did she have her surgery?" she asked.

"I don't know the exact date, but I believe it was more than six months ago. I hear her long recovery was caused by her surgery on both hands at the same time. She just could not avoid using them from time to time during her process of recovery, especially when they began to get better but not fully recovered yet."

"That's understandable," said Lucia. "At home and at work, you just can't do anything without your hands."

"You may consider just doing one hand at a time so that you can use the other to some extent," said the Chair. "In this case, you can guarantee a faster recovery."

"But that could take up to a year!" said Lucia.

"What's more important than your hands?" he said. "Do not worry about your work. I have already hired a temporary worker who can work until you are able to use your hands and return to work. If you go over the time limit, you may just have to switch to long-term disability benefits and be paid by the insurance company. That's all."

"Thank you so much for your kind advice," said Lucia, who thought she knew what to do now.

She felt it was unnecessary to call the other two colleagues for more advice, but, to her, a year of recovery was simply a luxury that she could not afford. The paramount issue still lay with her children. They just could not do without her hands for a year—not even for a month or a week!

Finding an alternative to surgery was her only option. Strangely, before finding her solution, she already felt a weight had been lifted from her shoulders, though she was still upset that she was one of the 2.3 million Canadians who suffer from repetitive strain injuries.

Lucia collapsed onto her sofa as soon as she finished talking with her Chair. At this moment, Ted, another colleague from the college called. Lucia began to pour out her grievances, worries, and concerns as soon as they started talking.

"Look, Lucia," said Ted sympathetically, "have you ever considered acupuncture treatment?"

"No. But could acupuncture really do me any good?" said Lucia. "Could the tiny needles have real effect on my intolerable numbness and pain? I have numbness and pain all over my lousy, clumsy arms."

"You never know unless you try," he said. "In fact, I have been receiving acupuncture treatments for my back pain and other problems. And it works just great on me. Most of my pains have disappeared after seven treatments."

"Really?" screamed Lucia. "Who is your acupuncturist?"

"Dr. Liu. He is a worldwide acupuncturist. He used to work in China and then Hungary. All the patients I know love him and speak highly of him. He has cured so many patients our mainstream doctors couldn't cure."

"Wow! I'd love to try," she said, feeling as if she had found her alternative treatment, "though I am scared of the needles."

"They don't really hurt," said Ted.

Nervously, Lucia asked for Dr. Liu's phone number. Ted gave it to her before they continued with their conversation.

Lucia needed no further persuasion. As soon as they finished talking, she called Dr. Liu in Regina and made an appointment with him in the afternoon. Her first meeting with him convinced her that he was the knowledgeable, competent acupuncturist she was looking for.

Dr. Liu conducted a pulse test for her, after which, he started telling her what her problems were: muscle tightness and stiffness in the upper body, neck, and arms; weak immune system; lack of energy; cold feet and hands; anxiety and poor sleep.

Lucia was impressed that he knew about her problems without being told. Then, they continued to discuss the treatments and how long it would take to cure the ailments. Dr. Liu suggested fifteen days of treatment, once daily, and then the condition would disappear.

She started her first treatment on the same visit. "I felt nervous about the needles," said Lucia afterward. She thought they would hurt her like sewing needles, but she found them to be painless.

Lucia started to notice relief after three treatments. The numbness, the pain, and the tingling in her hands and arms were gone after four treatments. Then, the stiffness in her neck and upper body also disappeared, and within a few days, she experienced more movement and rotation of the neck than she had in the past five years. Dr. Liu even treated her cold, from which she noticed she recovered much faster than previous ones.

"After experiencing these positive results, I would have acupuncture treatments for anything else that I was diagnosed with," she said in her letter of appreciation written for Dr. Liu.

Instead of a year, Lucia's alternative treatment took only fifteen days. Of the hundreds and thousands of carpal tunnel patients in Canada, she is one of the fortunate few who have escaped surgery without having to suffer chronic pain and numbness in her hands and arms, and stiffness in her neck and shoulders.

She went back to work in the third week with no pain or numbness anywhere in her body. How grateful she was to Dr. Liu for his acupuncture treatments that had cured all her ailments and therefore saved her from a much-feared surgical procedure.

Encounter at a Party

"Oh Dear! Here comes Dr. Liu!" screamed Macy, who was about to announce the end of her one-year-old son's birthday party at Metro Buffet Restaurant when she caught sight of a professional-looking man in a white gown who had come to buy his lunch. "Dr. Liu," she said in excitement, taking a large stride toward him, "what a happy surprise to see you here!" She grasped his hand, then turned to the partygoers and shouted at the top of her voice, "Hello everyone! Here is Dr. Liu!"

Everyone fixed their eyes on the doctor.

"I'd like to introduce Dr. Liu to you!" A loud applause was heard followed by silence. Macy moistened her lips and started speaking, sweeping her eyes across the audience sitting at the dining tables.

"My son owes his life to Dr. Liu. I owe my son to Dr. Liu. My husband owes his happy wife and lovely son to Dr. Liu. Our family owes everything to Dr. Liu!" Everyone could see her tears flickering in the chandelier light. "I am not a poet. I am not a writer. But I'd love to tell you my story. I am not a good storyteller, but I'll tell you exactly what happened to me eight years ago." She paused, looked at Dr. Liu, and then said to the partygoers, "Does everyone want to listen to my story?"

"Yes, we do!" they shouted in chorus.

Wiping her tears with her sleeve, Macy narrated a string of emotional events as follows:

"In 2003, at the age of thirty-two, I was diagnosed with a 1 cm by 1 cm uterine fibroid. I became really worried about it because I wanted to have a baby. But my family doctor told me that it was a small fibroid that posed no danger. She also told me that it was quite common for women to have benign tumors in the uterus. She neither prescribed any medications for me nor recommended any other treatment. As such, I went on with my life, as if everything was normal, but things were not normal. In 2006, I had another hysteroscopy, which showed my largest fibroid had grown to be 5.2 cm by 4.9 cm. Now I was three years older, and my fibroids had become five times as big. My family doctor apologized for failing to control the condition for me, saying that I might need surgery. I got really scared. I was not only scared of surgery but also of what might become of me afterward. Did it mean I would lose part of my womb— or all of it? Could I have babies after the surgery? Would a woman without a womb still be a woman? What did a wife without a womb mean to her husband? The more I thought, the more desperate I felt. Then, I decided I had to do something myself.

"I started searching for ways to control and improve my condition, hoping to reduce the size of the fibroids. First, I watched my diet carefully, eating the healthiest food and avoiding junk food altogether. Then, I purchased from the internet medicinal herbs prescribed for uterine fibroids. I did whatever I could, but all in vain. I noticed no improvement at all. To complicate my condition, I got pregnant in 2008, but due to various reasons, including anxiety and the existing fibroids in the uterus, I lost the fetus in the third month.

"As the common saying goes, mishaps do not come singly. Fed by the excess hormones during my pregnancy, my fibroids expanded rapidly—the largest one had grown to the size of 11 cm by 10 cm. Five months after my miscarriage, my belly still bulged out. Neighbors, friends, and colleagues thought I was pregnant again. What a cruel and embarrassing experience I had gone through! My obstetrician told me that I must avoid pregnancy until the condition improved significantly. His advice really burned me out. I was thirty-seven and, if I did not get pregnant within the next year or two, I would be running out of time. I started to look for my own solution again, this time, in real earnest. Then, on that lucky day, I came across an article about Dr. Liu, a well-known acupuncturist, whose patients had numerous successful treatment stories circulated in the media. His high morals, profound knowledge, and amazing success stories attracted me immediately. One of his proven skills was treating uterine fibroids! I did not fully believe the fibroid-treatment stories I read, and I was, in fact, scared of the acupuncture needles, but I had no choice. I didn't want to have my womb surgically removed. I wanted to have babies and I wanted my husband to be happy, so I decided to take a chance.

"I made an appointment with Dr. Liu and went to see him the following day. He gave me a pulse test and advised me to try a treatment period of fifteen days, forty minutes daily. I took his advice and started my treatment on the same day.

"What a miracle it was! During the fifteen days of treatment, I could see and feel my budging belly flattening day by day with the large lump underneath shrinking at the same time. After the first treatment period, my belly looked undeniably normal and healthy, though I could still feel a small lump underneath. For a thorough cure, I happily took another period of treatment, by the end of which I could not feel the lump anymore.

"Then, I saw my obstetrician who gave me another hysteroscopy. When the reports came, his assistant called me and informed me that my fibroids had improved greatly and that I could try to get pregnant again. When I asked about the sizes, she refused to tell me about them—perhaps they were all gone. She just assured me that I didn't have to worry about the condition anymore and that pregnancy was now safe for me. I stopped taking acupuncture treatments and gave my body a three-month break. During this break, I experienced no pain and no discomfort during my menstruation. The flow was also very normal. Most importantly, I felt no more lumps in the uterus. That convinced me I had really become a healthy wife again.

"Believing the time was right, my husband and I tried again in February 2009, and blessed by God, I got pregnant again. My new pregnancy went well, and my healthy son was born in October. A new life, a new member, had come into our family. Joy filled me and my husband from head to toe; our son's sweet crying and then giggling could be heard from bed to bath. You can't imagine how happy I was, being a mother!

"And here I am, celebrating my son's first birthday! My dear friends and relatives, won't you agree that my son owes his life to Dr. Liu? Won't you agree that I owe my son to Dr. Liu? Won't you agree that my husband owes his happy wife and lovely son to Dr. Liu? I am sure you agree with me that our happy family owes everything to Dr. Liu!

"Thank you again as ever, Dr. Liu!"

No sooner had she finished her story than she threw her arms around him. The amazed audience burst into cheers, standing in ovation for Dr. Liu's contribution to Macy's happy family.

Treating an Alzheimer's Patient

I flicked the first needle into his most important acupoint. This flick-insertion method was invented by me, and usually it is not that painful.

"Ouch," he cried when I flicked in the second needle. Probably it had touched the capillaries underneath his skin, but soon he calmed down.

When I flicked in the third, again it touched the capillaries. He threw a sudden kick at me but missed me. "No!" he shouted in anger.

I stopped. Dean Logan of the TCM College, who was with me at the university health center, asked me if I wanted to put another needle at another of Mr. Gore's acupoints, but I said no. "It's his first day. It doesn't matter if he receives less treatment. What matters most is his cooperation. We can gradually increase the treatment later." With his wife holding his hands, Mr. Gore immediately fell asleep. I was surprised that he fell asleep so quickly.

It turned out that Mrs. Gore had given him a sleeping pill before he came, in fear he would not cooperate with me. But for the best treatment results, I asked her not to give him any more sleeping pills next time. Forty minutes later, I removed the needles from Mr. Gore, thus completing the first treatment. In a way, he cooperated, but obviously due to the sleeping pill.

I had laid out a three-step approach to his treatment: first, have his cooperation; second, stop the deterioration of his disease; and third, start his recovery. "Treating Mr. Gore requires patience," I said to myself. "He is a highly educated man and a reputed scholar. We can't force him to do anything against his will."

For his second treatment, I gave him only one needle, which went into the most important acupoint that controlled the entire nerve system. He cooperated fully. I had asked Mrs. Gore not to give him any sleeping pill, but she said he would not cooperate with me without it. I stressed that for the best results, she must not give him any more medications before he came for the third treatment. I assured her that I would be able to secure his cooperation.

On November 30, they came again, and again I asked Mrs. Gore if she had given him any sleeping pill. She said no this time. Mr. Charlton, the TCM doctor of the health center, was assisting me. We asked Mr. Gore to lie down on the acupuncture bed. I told him that I was trying to help him regain his memory and that, when the needle went into his acupoint, it might just feel like a mosquito bite.

"Good," he said.

Soon all the five needles were flicked into his acupoints without mishap. I saw no abnormal reaction from the patient, so I signaled Mrs. Gore, who was holding his hand, to sit on the chair behind her. Then, Dr. Charlton and I left Mr. Gore to rest. We chatted outside, but two minutes later, I heard noises inside.

I lifted the door curtain only to see Mr. Gore standing on the floor. He had gotten off the treatment bed, and his wife was trying to push him back. I dashed in, followed by Dr. Charlton. With much talking and some shoving, we finally had him back on the bed. I gave him some additional massage on another acupoint, while Mrs. Gore rubbed his eye sockets, hoping to close his eyes. Dr. Charlton was massaging his right hand, but Mr. Gore was still restless. It was quite an effort for us to hold him there until the end of his treatment.

Twenty minutes later, I looked at my watch and said, "Fine. He has had enough treatment today." I quickly removed all his needles. Mr. Gore was silent, but he was really agitated. He had lost his temper, his face reddening. He made a fist and said, "Bang! Bang!"

"No bang, no bang, please!" said his wife.

Afterward, I asked her what "bang" meant, and she told me that he wanted to punch someone. Fortunately, I had been kind to him, and so he did not attack me. Mrs. Gore apologized, but I said, "That's one of the symptoms of his disease. If they would cooperate like other patients, then they wouldn't need any treatment."

Mr. Gore came again on December 2, again without taking any medications. I asked Mrs. Gore if she had seen any change in his behavior.

"Yes. After the last treatment, he seems to have changed in some ways," she said. "Sometimes he would pick up a book, intending to read it. He had not touched a book for a very long time."

I was overjoyed to hear about his improvement. Then, I asked him to lie down on the bed for treatment. He cooperated fully, and all my five needles were flicked into his acupoints without interruption or mishap. To our disbelief, Mr. Gore closed his eyes as he lay there quietly. Seeing this, his wife smiled at me, raising her thumb at me to show her happiness.

Forty minutes later, I came to remove his needles, surprised to find Mr. Gore awake, his eyes wide open. When I told him I was going to remove the needles, he said, "Yes." I was so happy with his treatment, and so were his wife and Dr. Charlton. At this point in time, I thought I must have been assisted and blessed by the Almighty. Mr. Gore was finally cooperating, and we would soon start regular treatment. The only problem was that he could not come for optimal frequency of treatment, which is no less than three times per week.

When he came on December 6, Mrs. Gore told me his condition had improved further—he wanted to say something, but he could not say it aloud. He fully cooperated with me again during the treatment. But the following day, Mrs. Gore told me that he had a stomachache, resulting in difficult bowel movements, which really irritated him. Mrs. Gore had taken him to a doctor of Western medicine, and they had to wait for him for about thirty minutes, and that caused her husband distress. Then, he came for acupuncture treatment, so he was not as gentle and cooperative as he had been the day before.

When I asked him if he wanted to have more acupuncture treatment, he said, "No!" We tried our best to persuade him to cooperate with us, but he kept saying no, until we finally gave up.

On December 12, he cooperated with me quite well in the beginning, but two of the needles might have gone a little deeper, causing him to scream, "Oh my!" But then he became quiet, closed his eyes, and fell asleep. Mrs. Gore, who had been holding his hands for ten minutes, then withdrew hers and began to read her magazine. Thirty-five minutes later, Mr. Gore got up, wanting to pull out the needles himself. It was time for me to remove his needles anyway, so I immediately started to do so. Mr. Gore did not really cooperate in the end: he pulled out one himself and gave it to me when I had just removed the other four.

Mrs. Gore told me she had pain on her right shoulder, so I picked up a new needle and give her some treatment. Meanwhile, I asked Mr. Gore, who was standing beside her, "Did you like your acupuncture treatment today?"

"No!" he said, punching me on the chest with moderate force.

"Quite a strong man, aren't you?" I teased him.

"Why did you do that!" Mrs. Gore scolded him.

"Never mind," I said to her. "He is ill and he doesn't know what he is doing."

Despite all the small incidents and interruptions, Mr. Gore's treatment continued until he began to say two-syllable words to me, like "okay" and "bye-bye," which was a breakthrough compared with his original monosyllabic words, such as "yeah," "yes," and "no."

After a few more treatments, when I asked him, "Are you cold?" he was able to say, "I am not cold."

When I asked him, "How are you doing?" he would say, "I am okay." Alternatively, he might say, "I am good."

On January 11, 2012, I was about to flick the needles into his acupoints, when Mr. Gore suddenly got off his bed and said, "No acupuncture treatment!" I tried my best to ask him to lie on the treatment bed, but he just would not cooperate. "Why have you become like this again?" his wife reproached him.

"Never mind," I said. "We can try again next time."

Mrs. Gore looked disappointed.

"Mr. Gore seems to understand everything now," I said to her.

"Yes, indeed. He understands everything. Very well," she said. "He's now able to write his own name, which he hadn't been able to do for many years. He can also write the ten numbers: 1, 2, 3, 4, 5, 6, 7, 8, 9, 0. And he is able to pick his own clothes now. Yesterday, he was looking for clothes in the closet and chose the right suit for himself. He used to take anything within reach and often put on my dresses."

Mr. Gore, a world-renowned physicist, used to be a man of intelligence and creativity. He had won many prestigious awards and was highly respected throughout the world. Unfortunately, he was diagnosed with Alzheimer's disease in 2003, and had been battling it without satisfactory success.

For a 75-year-old Alzheimer's patient who had suffered the disease for nine years, his improvement was a miracle. Again, I thanked the Almighty for the unbelievable changes that had taken place in him.

15 Years of Allergies Cured in 20 Days

Bob, his wife Lisa, and their three-year-old son arrived in the provincial park early in the afternoon. They had come for camping on the Victoria Day long weekend. It was a pastime everyone in his family enjoyed, especially in late spring and early summer. But today, before Bob could set up their tent under the big trees, water suddenly started gushing out of his eyes and nose. When he looked at himself, he found red rashes all over his body. Feeling itchy and in pain, Bob put down the tent and walked to the green meadow near the brook, worried that he might have to cancel the trip.

"Do you have an allergy, Bob?" Lisa asked.

"I never had this trouble before," he said. Then he shouted in panic, "Oh gosh! Could the powerful antibiotics have damaged my immune system? Oh my God!"

Bob looked distressed, almost certain it was the medications that had caused his allergy symptoms. Four weeks earlier, he had suffered a severe lung infection after he had caught the flu, for which he was given an injection of the most powerful antibiotics available. Then, he continued to take large doses of oral antibiotics for sixteen days until it was finally cured. He felt a little weak, but he had not expected any side effects.

Bob's condition was deteriorating rapidly. Soon, it became clear that he could not stay in the park any longer, so the family had to pack up and go home. What a disappointment it was, especially for their excited boy!

After the long weekend, Bob went to see an immunologist,

who tested him and found that he was allergic to more than ten things, including pollens, dust, mold, grasses, trees, flowers, and various types of food. But he was never allergic to any of them in the past.

"Could the antibiotics I took have caused my allergies?" he asked the immunologist.

"Not likely," said his doctor, who did not want to speculate.

"If so, could you reverse my immune system's aggressive attacks?" Bob asked.

"I don't know what has triggered your allergies. I only know that the tests show you are allergic to these items," said the specialist.

"When do you think my allergies will disappear?" Bob asked him on his fifth visit.

"Probably in twenty-five years," said the specialist.

"When should I come to see you again?" asked Bob.

"One year from now," the immunologist said, indicating there was no quick cure for him. Regardless, he prescribed some medications for Bob.

Soon Bob found there was no easy cure for allergies. The medications prescribed by the immunologist did not really work. They eased his ailments but did not cure them. Bob's eyes, nose, and throat bothered him the most when he went outdoors. His quality of life dropped drastically, as he could not enjoy any of the seasons except winter. Fall was the worst for him: he had to hide at home most of the time with the doors and windows tightly closed.

Bob sought additional treatments from other doctors. He tried all the effective treatments available, including daily oral medications, serum injected into his arm for five years, nasal injection for two years, but none of them worked to his satisfaction. The marginal improvement was not worth the inconvenience and pain of the treatments.

Five years later, he gave up treatments and medications, choosing to put up with his sneezing and runny eyes and nose, and instead live an inactive life. Soon, he even got used to his unhealthy way of living.

Time flew and fifteen years without outdoor pleasure activities passed—until he made a business trip to Alberta where he stayed in the same hotel with his colleague Shawn.

"You could try acupuncture," Shawn told him when he heard about his chronic allergies.

"I will think about it," said a hesitant Bob, skeptical of acupuncture's efficacy. Also, he did not like anyone sticking needles into his body. Thus, he continued with his usual, unhealthy life.

Then came his company's important event—the golf tournament taking place in Avonlea the day before Mother's Day. It was an annual social activity he hated to miss. Bob loved golf and was good at it, so he decided to join his colleagues.

What he did not know was that the invisible brute was waiting to ambush him in the open. His allergies got worse with the start of the tournament. When it ended, he was not the same person anymore. His eyes kept watering, his nose was running nonstop. The allergy spray he had brought along could not stop the allergy attack.

He finally made it home, but the unleashed beast showed no sign of retreating. Bob kept wiping his eyes and nose until they became red and raw. On Mother's Day, he tried to get up, but he just could not. The moment he sat up, water would gush out of his eyes and nose. When he looked in the mirror, he was unable to recognize himself—his eyes were two red bulging sockets; his nose was swollen and raw. He was also suffering an unbearable headache and breathing coarsely. He had to lie in bed to ease the condition.

During these difficult moments, Bob thought of his conversation with Shawn on the business trip to Alberta two weeks earlier. Both he and Lisa thought he should contact the acupuncturist Shawn had mentioned. Obviously, life was not very pleasant for Bob, and it needed improvement, especially when assistance was available.

"Shawn, my allergies are getting really bad," he said to him, when he went back to work the following morning. "Could you give me the acupuncturist's contact information?"

Glancing at Bob's eyes and nose, Shawn knew how sick Bob was. He quickly found the information and gave it to him. After learning about Dr. Liu's credentials, Bob became more confident in acupuncture treatment. He contacted Dr. Liu without delay, making an appointment for that evening.

After giving him a pulse test and looking at his tongue, Dr. Liu told Bob, "Your allergy is curable. I have treated patients with your symptoms."

"How long will it take?" asked Bob.

"You likely need fifteen treatments, one per day. Each treatment takes about forty-five minutes. I will give you the first treatment right now if you decide to stay."

Bob decided to start his treatment immediately, thinking that he would try a little while and see what happened. Bob survived the first treatment. The tiny needle did not hurt as badly as he thought it would.

"How do you feel?" Dr. Liu asked him after the first treatment.

"Pretty good," said Bob, out of courtesy, still rather skeptical. After five or six treatments, he really began to feel better, but he was still not fully convinced that his positive feeling was entirely due to Dr. Liu's treatments. After two more treatments, he could no longer deny the efficacy of his acupuncture treatments. To confirm this, he asked other patients in Dr. Liu's clinic how they felt. They all said that they were feeling wonderful and had so much energy, just like how he felt.

"Acupuncture does seem to work," Bob said to himself. "It may be my cure. I'll stay the course and see what happens." With confidence, he decided to complete the entire fifteen treatments.

"Dr. Liu, I have been taking some nose spray prescribed by my other doctor," he told him. "Should I stop using it?"

"Don't quit it just yet, not until your immune system is strong enough," said Dr. Liu. "I also have some Chinese herbal medication that can help improve your condition."

"Can I buy it from you then?" Bob asked.

"You don't need it for now," said Dr. Liu.

After twelve treatments, Bob felt he had become a new person, strong and healthy. "I can wrestle an alligator now," he told Lisa. He even went out and played golf again, walking eighteen holes with the golf clubs on his shoulders. He enjoyed his outdoor activities to his heart's content. "That was something I had not done in so many years," he told Lisa, who was shocked and worried that the open air could have easily ruined his acupuncture treatments.

"Oh, Bob! But are you all right?" she said.

"I am perfectly fine, honey," said Bob. "I didn't have any allergic reaction at all," he assured her.

"But please go slowly, Bob," she said lovingly, pleased that she had urged him to see the acupuncturist on Mother's Day.

After the initial fifteen treatments, Bob said that he was feeling excellent in all aspects, but Dr. Liu suggested he take five more, just to consolidate the positive results. It was for his own good, so Bob happily took the advice. On his last visit, he asked Dr. Liu when he should return for a follow-up treatment.

"You shouldn't have to come back at all. At least, not this year," said Dr. Liu. "Next year maybe. Come back only if you become sick again, but I doubt you will really need to."

"How about the Chinese medicine you mentioned on my first day of treatment?" Bob asked.

"No. You don't need it," Dr. Liu said.

In fact, Bob had stopped his allergy medications after his thirteenth treatment, and he had taken none at all since, but he remained healthy and energetic every day.

Now, Bob feared neither grasses, trees, and flowers nor dirt and mold. In the following week, he undertook the heavy task of re-landscaping his backyard without wearing a mask, a job he dared not even think about in the past ten years. On the weekend, he confidently went camping in the provincial park again with his family, tenting in the grass under the trees. How happy his family was! Finally, they were enjoying their family pastime again after they had missed it for fifteen long years.

Bob, who had suffered the pain of chronic allergies, truly appreciated the joy and happiness of an allergy-free life. Indeed, he was a lucky one who happened to have a coworker who knew about Dr. Liu, who in twenty days cured all the allergies that Bob had suffered for fifteen years.

Not a Doctor but a Deity

I met Dr. Liu in his clinic during his lunch break last Wednesday to verify the treatment details of three of his previous patients. After reminding him of the purpose of my visit, I helped myself to the chair at his diagnosis desk where he usually received his new patients. Aware of his busy schedule, I said that, to keep my visit as short as possible, if he agreed, I would just read him a summary of each patient's story that I had prepared and then pause for his corrections of inaccurate details, if any.

He nodded in agreement, so I started immediately.

"The first story is about your 13-year-old patient who suffered facial droop. As a result, her face became contorted. Its muscles were stiff, exposing the unpretty inner eyelids. She could not move her eyes; neither could she swallow food and water graciously. When she tried to eat, her food and beverages would fall out of the corner of her mouth. Even at night while she was sleeping, her eyes still did not close. She was no longer the beautiful girl she used to be, and she could not go to school.

"She burst into uncontrollable sobs after looking in the mirror. The whole family was devastated. Her desperate mother, Ms. Chauffer, took her to her conventional doctor, who prescribed medications for her daughter's facial palsy but also warned her of the various severe side effects. Ms. Chauffer thought it was too risky for the child, so she opted for alternative medicine. She took her to an acupuncturist who gave her treatment without delay, but the child felt no positive effect after the initial treatment. The frantic mother continued to seek effective treatment for her beloved daughter. As luck had it, by evening time, she found you, Dr. Liu. She highly respected you, adored you, and had confidence in you. Therefore, she sought immediate treatment from you. You accepted the young patient and gave her the first acupuncture treatment that same evening. To her delight and relief, her daughter felt better immediately after the first treatment. After another four treatments, her facial palsy was almost all gone. After her course of fifteen treatments, she completely recovered from her illness.

"No one could notice any trace of the young patient's facial palsy. The whole family was astounded by your miraculous acupuncture treatment. They were drowned in tears of happiness and gratitude. Long after, when Ms. Chauffer was sharing her daughter's successful acupuncture story with the media, she still could not hold back her grateful tears.

"Ms. Chauffer chose to go public because she hoped that other parents would know whom to look to if their children suffered the same crisis. She told everyone that your effective treatment won her utmost admiration and heartfelt thanks, and your ethical standards are the highest among those she knew about. Is my summary of the 13-year-old patient's story accurate, Dr. Liu?"

"The patient's illness you have described is accurate, as I remember," said the doctor, "and so were the results of my treatment."

"Dr. Liu, the second patient I want to verify with you is 41-year-old Ms. Wayna, who had severe menstrual problems due to hormonal imbalance. She had this condition for approximately a year and a half. She started with a milder condition, but she was busy and just ignored it, until the following June when it suddenly deteriorated, resulting in hemorrhaging that caused her fatigue and dizziness, which kept her from work. Several months of treatment with Western and Chinese medications yielded no positive results.

"Then, as the story goes, she found you, and you told her you could cure her illness. In the same conversation, you told her that three to five treatments would stop the bleeding, but a thorough cure would require one or two courses of treatment. Though she was skeptical, she came to you for a try. To her delight, her bleeding improved after just the first treatment. After three treatments, it completely stopped, and she had no bleeding for nine days. Her husband, in disbelief, said, 'Dr. Liu is not a doctor but a deity,' by which he meant you were the best of the best, next to God but above all the other acupuncturists.

"Then, Ms. Wayna's friends came to visit her from overseas. Thus, she forewent her treatment to entertain them, busying herself from morning till night. They had a wonderful time, but when her guests left, her bleeding started again. This time, it was much worse than ever before. Panic-stricken, Ms. Wayna went to see her conventional doctor, who prescribed hormone treatment to balance her system. After taking the medications, her bleeding stopped briefly, but then it burst out again due to the medication's side effects.

"With few options available, the desperate patient came back to you. You told her, 'Stay and do acupuncture. Not every doctor is able to cure this type of illness. You need rest, in addition to treatment.' You warned her, 'Exhausting yourself will cause your condition to relapse.' You also told her that you had done extensive treatment research in China, for which you had won a research award. This time, she cooperated fully, never missing a treatment throughout the two courses of treatment. For three months after her completion of treatment, she told you her menstrual cycles had been normal, and she was again living a healthy, happy life. Dr. Liu, is this an accurate summary of Ms. Wayna's story?"

"Yes, it is," said Dr. Liu. "Your narration of her previous treatments by other medical practitioners is what I have heard about. And your account of my treatments that finally cured her illness is also accurate."

"Then, there is your 30-year-old patient by the name of Jody who has told a news reporter, 'Dr. Liu is a miracle doctor. I have two boys and I want a girl. But I had a problem with my period. Early yesterday, I told Dr. Liu that I had not had a period for forty-five days. He told me that he would treat me and then my period would come very soon. He treated me in the afternoon, and my period came in the evening. It was miraculous!' Is it true that you restarted her menstrual flow with just one acupuncture treatment?"

"Yes, I did," said Dr. Liu.

I was impressed by the three patients' treatment stories he had confirmed. He had cured numerous patients who had many other unheard stories that would interest me and others. How I wished I could ask him to tell me more, but he had to attend to his patients. Finally, I expressed my heartfelt thanks to him and his patients who had generously made their stories available to the public.

Reluctantly I left him, still in disbelief that he was able to cure so many ailments that conventional medicine could not effectively cure despite so many years of continuous research and improvement in theory and practice.

Speechless

How exciting it would be! Her surgery would start soon. Then, she would not feel the lumps again! She opened the window of her ward in the Budapest hospital and heard birds singing sweetly on the trees.

Mrs. Banar, a well-educated lady in her fifties who had a sweet voice like a lark, had a condition known as thyroid nodules, which had been bothering her for ten years. Though they were benign and painless, the bumps at the base of her neck above the chest just did not feel good or look pretty. Three weeks earlier, she had a thorough discussion with her doctor, after which she decided to have them surgically removed once and for all.

When everything was taken care of, the head nurse told her husband, Dr. (PhD) Talars Banar, that they would look after his wife, so he could go home and attend to his own affairs. He thanked them but reminded them to call him should anything unexpected happen. He also said he wanted to be informed when the surgery was completed.

"Sure. We will call you," said the head nurse.

At 5:00 pm, the hospital called Dr. Banar and told him the surgery was successfully completed and everything was just fine, and that he could visit his wife the following morning.

"How is my wife doing?" Dr. Banar asked the nurse at the front desk the next morning when he was checking in to visit her.

"Perfect," she said. "She is doing just fine. We gave her liquid food this morning. In fact, she has just finished eating."

"Thank you all for your great care!" he said.

"You're most welcome! Okay, you can go in now," said the nurse. "She is in Room 3 on the right. I will take you there." As soon as they arrived at the ward, the nurse left.

"How are you doing, darling?" Dr. Banar asked as soon as his eyes met his wife's.

She shook her head, then nodded, but she remained silent.

Dr. Banar was confused. He did not know what she meant. "How are you feeling?" he said.

She pointed at her throat and shook her head. She was still silent.

"Just relax and try not to speak if it is too painful," he comforted her.

She pointed at his pen in his pocket. He understood that she wanted to write something, so he gave it to her with a piece of paper the size of a palm.

"I have lost my voice. I can't speak, and my throat is tight and sore," she wrote on the paper and gave it to him.

"Just relax and rest. I am sure the pain will be gone soon, and we can talk later." Dr. Banar left her to sleep. Then he spoke to the doctor in charge of the inpatient department and was told that it was a temporary condition that would disappear within two or three days. He went back to tell his wife, and she smiled and nodded at him.

The following day, when Dr. Banar visited his wife again, she told him her pain was getting better, but she still had to communicate with him through writing. She still could not say a word. Now both husband and wife became somewhat anxious and even a little worried, though neither said so.

On the third day, Mrs. Banar's pain was basically gone, but she could not find her voice. She had been trying to say something since she finished her breakfast. Each time she tried, she hoped she would at least hear herself making some noises, but she failed repeatedly. Dr. Banar became really worried now. He spoke with her chief physician again. The doctor did not try to comfort him this time. Neither did he say the condition would improve soon. He furrowed his eyebrows, as if baffled by something he did not understand.

"Oh God!" cried Dr. Banar unexpectedly. "Could my wife's vocal cords have been damaged during the surgery?"

"I don't know at this point in time," said the doctor. "We can only hope that it did not happen."

"Oh my God!" shouted Dr. Banar. "How could this have happened?"

"We will re-examine her and let you know the answer as soon as we can," the doctor said shamefacedly.

On the fifth day after her surgery, Mrs. Banar was given some antibiotic gel to apply to the stiches until her skin had fully recovered. For the average patient, that was the end of the procedure, but obviously not in Mrs. Banar's case. Regardless, she would be released from the hospital.

Mrs. Banar's life had changed completely. She could not speak anymore. She had to communicate in writing not only with her husband but also with the doctors, the nurses, and anyone else. When it became too time consuming, she simply switched to gestures, but the worst was yet to come.

"Mrs. Banar," the doctor in charge of her care finally informed her, "I regret to tell you that your vocal cords were damaged during the surgery. Honestly, I don't know how it happened, but the damage is permanent. We apologize for that."

Tears gushed from her eyes. "I don't want to live anymore," she cried to herself voicelessly as she sprang up from the hospital bed, dashing toward the window in desperation. The sounds of crashing glass scared the nurses and her husband, who was approaching her room. The doctor could not hear what she had said to herself, but he knew what she wanted to do. He was panicking now. Had the window not been barred, she would have jumped out and killed herself already.

"Mrs. Banar, please calm down. We are trying our best to

help you," he said, aware that there was nothing he and other doctors could do for her. He repeated the bad news about her damaged vocal cords to Dr. Banar, who reacted much more calmly than his wife.

Dr. Banar went up to her and hugged her, saying, "Darling, my friend Dr. Liu, the miracle acupuncturist, may be able to help you regain your speech ability. Let's just go home and ask him if he can do something for you."

"What a cruel joke the hospital has played on my wife," thought Dr. Banar. "How could such a simple surgery have ended up damaging my wife's vocal cords? How are we going to live our normal life from now on? Oh, help us, God!"

In desperation, Dr. Banar called Dr. Wan Cheng Liu and told him the mishap from beginning to end.

"It's curable," said Dr. Liu. "I can help you out of this crisis. Bring your wife to my clinic as soon as you can." And that was what Dr. Banar did.

Dr. Liu first calmed the patient down to prevent her from taking her own life. Then, he asked for her cooperation, which was to ensure she would receive the treatment required for a full recovery within the shortest time possible. A well-educated lady who was reasonable, respectful, and optimistic, Mrs. Banar cooperated with Dr. Liu fully.

Indeed, a miracle happened! After four weeks of acupuncture treatment, Mrs. Banar regained her ability to speak. At this unbelievable moment in her life, she remained speechless, not knowing what to say to Dr. Liu who had given her a second happy life.

Hearing her long-missed voice that was as sweet as a lark's, Mrs. Banar started sobbing uncontrollably.

Pride Put Aside

It was a usual Saturday morning, and 58-year-old Aylor Fay was opening the door of her antique store downtown. She turned on all the lights and switched on her cash register.

"Good morning." She smiled at a middle-aged man who was entering her store.

"Oh God!" cried the man. "Are you okay?" He saw Aylor crashing onto the tiled floor and tried to help her to her feet but failed.

"I can't move," she said, groaning in pain.

"What happened?" he asked. "Should I call the ambulance for you?"

"Please call my son, first," she said, reciting the phone number to him.

Her son was working in another store on the neighboring street, so it took him only two minutes to rush over. "Mom, what happened?" he said.

"I don't know, Peter," she said. "I cannot move. I feel numb and pain everywhere."

Peter called the ambulance immediately, which came quickly and took his mother to the hospital three blocks away. He followed behind.

"Thank God, Mom is still conscious." He breathed a sigh of relief after she checked in.

How fast life could change! Before she opened her store, Aylor was a healthy person, but within five minutes, she became someone who could not sit, stand, feed herself, or go to the washroom.

"Fortunately, she had no stroke," the doctor in the emergency room told Peter. "It is spondylitis, or inflammation in the spinal bones. Your mother has become paralyzed, but at least her brain is still good. That's why I said, 'Fortunately, she had no stroke.'"

"Oh gosh!" said a panicked Peter. "What are we to do?"

"She needs to be hospitalized," said the doctor. "We will do whatever we can for her. But I must tell you that there is no cure for severe spondylitis. There is a possibility she may be paralyzed permanently, depending on her condition."

As advised, Aylor was hospitalized. She had one blood test after another, followed by X-rays, then CT examinations, and so on and so forth. She took various medications and received physiotherapy. She was treated by internal physicians, neurologists, massage therapists, and chiropractors, among others. The doctors did everything they could, but Aylor's condition just did not improve.

"Do you think acupuncture may improve my mom's condition?" Peter asked the physician in charge of his mother's care ten months after she was hospitalized.

"Acupuncture will not help," said the doctor. "If the entire hospital cannot improve her condition, how could acupuncture be of any good to her?"

Peter left him, grumbling to himself: "If you can't do anything, why not give other medical practitioners a try?" But he just would not give up yet.

He raised the issue with the physician again the following day. "I really think we should bring in an acupuncturist to give my mom a try. I hear Dr. Liu from China is a very good one. He has cured many patients in Budapest and other places in Hungary."

"It's not because I don't like your idea, but it's a well-known fact that acupuncture cannot cure your mother's disease," said the doctor.

"If we don't give the acupuncturist a chance, how could we

know for sure?" said Peter.

"As you know, we have tried every treatment possible, and none worked! You would just be wasting your time and money. Besides, acupuncture may even make her worse." The doctor sounded impatient, so Peter said no more. He just did not want to offend him, for he would eventually need his permission to bring in Dr. Liu.

After Peter went home, he started collecting successful treatment stories about Dr. Liu's patients, published in Hungarian newspapers, magazines, and elsewhere. Then, he contacted Dr. Liu, who told him that his mother's illness was curable and that he was willing to treat her if the hospital granted him the permission.

The next morning, Peter approached the chief physician again. "Sir, I had a quick search yesterday and found many news stories about the genius acupuncturist who has cured many rare diseases in Hungary." With this, he showed him ten of the stories he had printed.

"Don't believe these stories without real proof and facts. There are stories and stories about successful treatments, even successful cancer treatments. But do you really believe them?" The doctor still did not want to give Peter permission.

"Sir, what do you have to lose?" said Peter. "You cannot do anything for my mother. She has been under your care for ten months, and she is as bad as she was ten months ago! I insist that you kindly grant us the permission to bring in Dr. Liu to give my mother acupuncture treatment!"

"Since you stubbornly insist, I agree, but you and the acupuncturist have to sign the legal documents, as required by the rules and regulations. If anything happens, you and the acupuncturist will be responsible. Neither the hospital nor the doctors and nurses will share any of such liability."

"That's fine," said Peter. "We will sign all the papers you want us to sign."

Thus, the signing of the papers began, followed by Dr. Liu's immediate treatment. To the amazement of the Hungarian doctors and nurses, Dr. Liu inserted his silvery needles by flicking each into the acupoint in an almost artistic way. How skillful he was and how confident he looked!

After a month of Dr. Liu's treatment, Aylor was able to get off bed and even walk, albeit with support. The Hungarian doctors were left in disbelief. All pride and prejudice put aside, they went up to shake hands with Dr. Liu. "Congratulations! You've done the impossible!"

"Thank you." Dr. Liu smiled. Aylor's healing was well within his expectation.

What the Hungarian doctors had yet to know was that Aylor later fully recovered, able to walk without support. Then, she resumed her vibrant life, operating her busy antique store downtown as ever before.

"How lucky I am," she would say to conclude her story when anyone asked about her difficult recovery.

Is It Fate?

I sit here in front of my desk, thinking about two people: Jason Martin in Toronto, who is my friend May's husband, and Nora Schollen, Dr. Liu's patient in Regina. Like two million other Canadians (estimated by the Canadian Chiropractic Association), they had to limit activities due to back injuries. Jason and Nora started to feel back pain about twenty years ago, but their life is not the same today.

I met Jason at a dinner party hosted by our mutual friend, Ivory, in a North York restaurant in the summer of 1996. He was a healthy man working as a property manager for an apartment building in Scarborough, but when we met again in the same restaurant the following year, he complained about back pain. Since back pain was a common ailment, none of us recommended any treatment option for him. Like many others, we thought his pain would disappear after a proper rest or through massage or some other easily accessible treatment.

However, Jason's condition did not improve. When Ivory invited us to another summer get-together in 1998, May said that Jason's back pain was debilitating and that he might not be able to attend. To our relief, in the end Jason still showed up. At least, it indicated that he was still able to move about, but he looked pale and weak. He moved about slowly and carefully, seeming to avoid bumping into anyone or anything. It was a sign of a hurting spine. When your spine hurts, you cannot even stand straight, let alone lift and carry anything heavy.

I skipped the gathering in 1999 because I was busy

preparing for my daughter's birth. And then in 2000, we found out that Jason could not come to our annual dinner anymore. His back pain was just unbearable, and he could not even get off his bed. Ivory and I were sad when May, who had come alone, broke the news at the table. The dinner was not the same without Jason, and we have had no more summer dinners ever since.

I called May several times after our last gathering, only to hear disappointing news.

"Jay doesn't get any better. He is in bed most of the time," May told me when I called them the following year. Then, when I called her nine months later, she said, "Jason's in great pain. He suffers day and night. He can't even sleep properly. The doctor said he needs surgery."

Half a year after his surgery, I hoped to hear positive news from her when I called again, but again I was disappointed. "The surgery was not very successful." May burst into sobs. "Jason has to lie in bed permanently now." I dared not call May again, because I could not do anything for Jason, and each time I called, I seemed to make her even sadder. Simply, I was helpless, May was helpless, and Ivory was helpless. I kept wondering if something could have been done to save Jason's back before his surgery.

Jason knows Chinese, so he could have found alternative treatment if he wanted to. He could have tried acupuncture treatment. Or he could have quit his property management job, which was literally a labor job, unsuitable for him because he used to be a college teacher for many years and was not strong enough for it. But it was all too late. His surgery had been done, so he had become permanently disabled.

And here is the story about Nora Schollen who started to feel the same back pain at about the same time as Jason did, but she opted for alternative treatment that resulted in different efficacy. To cut the story short, at the crucial moment when Nora was suffering unbearable back pain, her husband mentioned her condition to Yvonne, who had never met her but came to her rescue by giving her the contact information of Dr. Liu, a world-renowned acupuncturist, who was treating patients in Regina at the time.

In fact, Nora was skeptical in the beginning, and like most patients, she was scared of the needles. Nonetheless, she bravely tried Dr. Liu's acupuncture treatment. As she told Yvonne in her thank-you email, she was extremely nervous throughout her first session of treatment, and Dr. Liu had to tell her to relax from beginning to end.

But just as the common saying goes, no pain, no gain. It is believed that relaxed patients with a higher level of confidence in themselves and in the doctor experience positive results faster than the nervous ones who lack confidence. In Nora's case, she courageously received her treatment, but felt no relief for the entire first week, which also indicated how stubborn her chronic pain was and how difficult the recovery process could be and how important her cooperation was. But she did not give up.

"Then, all of a sudden, it happened; the pain just went away," she told Yvonne. Her unendurable pain was cured in two weeks.

After her pain disappeared, Nora went on holidays, during which she slept on a foam pad instead of a mattress. Realizing it was not the best thing for her when she got up in the morning, she thought she might have spoiled the positive results of Dr. Liu's acupuncture treatment. She expected the familiar pain to return, but it did not. She continued to be a healthy, happy lady with a strong back, and has remained so since.

Jason and Nora were patients with the same condition of chronic back pain starting at about the same time. Both suffered until intervention seemed inevitable, but Jason ended up being bedridden permanently, while Nora fully recovered and became a pain-free, healthy person again.

The irony is that Jason knows the Chinese language and

could readily search for alternative treatment, which he had not tried, while Nora, who knows no Chinese, was able to find a renowned Chinese-speaking acupuncturist who cured her illness without leaving any sequelae.

I keep wondering: Is that fate? Is there such a thing as fate? If not, could we believe that what one chooses affects how one lives?

An Apology to Dr. Liu

It was 5:00 p.m. on a breezy, sunny summer Sunday. Inside the Century Palace Restaurant across from Dr. Liu's acupuncture clinic sat three of his ex-patients, Lynda Jengjerd, Rosa Chang, and Carol German. They had placed a large birthday cake on the restaurant table. Then, Carol went across the corridor and instantly came back with their doctor.

"Happy birthday!" the three ladies shouted in chorus, as Carol showed him to his seat.

"Wow," said Dr. Liu, surprised that they even knew his birthday. "Thank you! But—"

"Happy birthday to you..." The ladies stood up and started singing, clapping their hands to the beat of the song. The nearby patrons sitting around them joined in the singing and clapping. It was such a jubilant occasion. When the singing ended, they applauded another minute. The other patrons did not know who the important man was, but they knew he must be someone very special. They craned their necks and fixed their eyes on Dr. Liu, eager to know more about him.

"Dr. Liu, we have gathered here for two purposes today," Carol announced. "One is to thank you again for your miraculous acupuncture treatments. The second is to express our sincere apology."

"Thank you for all this," said Dr. Liu. "I appreciate everything here—the beautiful song you have just sung, this beautiful birthday cake, and all these delicious-looking dishes, but why an apology?"

"There is something we never told you," Rosa joined in.

"We all feel guilty about it. We have been feeling guilty about it every time we think of it. And it has been so many years."

"So, today," Lynda picked up Rosa's thread of conversation, "we want to confess our guilt so that we will have a clear conscience from now on."

"Ladies, I am still confused," said Dr. Liu. "You have done nothing wrong. You were wonderful patients."

They looked at one another for a moment. Lynda frowned; Rosa bit her lips; Carol cleared her voice and broke the silence. "Dr. Liu, in fact, we were not perfect patients in the first place. Every one of us was skeptical about your acupuncture treatment in the beginning. To be honest with you, we did not really think that acupuncture would cure our diseases. We all tried, just because we had no better options than acupuncture."

"And that's it?" laughed Dr. Liu.

"We are embarrassed that we still remained skeptical even when your initial treatments showed positive results," Carol continued. "Only when our ailments significantly improved or totally disappeared, did we have real confidence in you. Only when our ultrasound reports and other hard data confirmed the miraculous treatments really yielded undeniable positive results did we truly believe in you."

"That's perfectly all right." Dr. Liu nodded, as if he was thinking about something. "You are not alone. Almost every one of my patients has the same experience. But thank you for being frank." He paused. Then, he swept his eyes across the table, saying, "How is everyone doing?"

"We are doing great!" said Lynda. "Since you gave me the acupuncture treatments six years ago, my high blood pressure dropped to normal and it has been regular ever since. I haven't had any dizziness or headaches since. I have been enjoying working and living a happy life with my family."

"How about you, Rosa? I remember you are from Hong Kong. Have you got used to the cold weather here?" asked the doctor.

"Life could not have been better, Dr. Liu," said Rosa. "If you remember, I was diagnosed with a 4 cm by 3 cm by 3 cm cyst on the right ovary, and then another cyst measuring 2.3 cm on the left. They had been causing pain and discomfort and other problems, which I hate to repeat, until I sought treatment from you. You told me ovarian cysts were relatively easy to cure, but my other doctors failed to bring them under control, until I came to you ten years ago. You cured all my ovarian cysts after fifteen treatments. I have been very healthy since. I own a fashion business in Toronto. Now I have two great kids aged three and four."

"How wonderful!" Dr. Liu smiled. Then he looked at Carol.

"Dr. Liu," she said slowly, "as you know, I am not as lucky as they are."

"Never mind," Dr. Liu said, seeming to suggest that she avoid the conversation topic, but Carol did not stop.

"Unfortunately," Carol continued, "I was diagnosed with that malignant tumor in the breast. It's been a dark shadow in my life since."

"Try not to think about it. Just go on living your life, your happy life," Dr. Liu said.

"Thank you!" said Carol. "That was what you told me five years ago. And again, I want to thank you for the effective treatment you gave me then. I had been suffering from all kinds of illnesses for seven years before I came to you. The different treatments I had received in the hospital had nearly ruined my health. First, I had a double mastectomy. Then, I received the chemotherapy that caused such reaction to my system—it resulted in my loss of hair and early menopause that caused insomnia, hot flashes, depression, memory loss, concentration problems, along with low energy, weight gain, and numbness in my hands and feet. The list goes on. Then, you gave me acupuncture treatment. The best part of it was I did not need to take any more medications. There were no side effects of any type. We all know my disease is incurable, but after the first period of treatment, one session daily for the first week, and then once every other day for two weeks, my health improved dramatically. The treatments greatly improved my energy level and my quality of sleep. I had also lost ten pounds by the end of that treatment period."

Due to the nature of her disease, Dr. Liu did not smile anymore. "I am glad the treatment worked for you," he said, unable to find other words to comfort her.

"On the bright side, my condition has been under control. I have been living a normal life without mishaps ever since," Carol concluded.

"I am so glad to hear all your success stories," said Dr. Liu, again, sweeping his eyes across the ladies sitting in front of him.

"Cheers!" Lynda raised her orange glass, joined by the other ladies. Dr. Liu picked up his glass as well. "Many happy returns of the day, Dr. Liu!"

"Cheers," they said in chorus, as they heard unexpected clapping around their table. The other restaurant patrons around them, who had overheard their touching stories, felt immensely proud of Dr. Liu, who had made such a difference in his patients' lives.

Before departure, Carol asked, "Dr. Liu, have you forgiven us for our guilt, for being skeptical about your treatment in the beginning?"

"My dear ladies, forget it! It's not an issue," Dr, Liu assured them. "As I said just now, all my patients are like that. That is why Harry J. Huang often says, 'Experiencing is believing.'"

The three ladies and the other patrons burst into a furious applause.

Legs Nearly Lost

George Goodwill, the editor of *Community News*, stares with profound interest at Mr. Loudon's "Letter to the Editor" submitted for consideration of publication in his newspaper. The event it describes is none of those vicious rapes, violent kidnappings, or brutal killings, but it carries a hidden message between the lines: alternative medicine deserves recognition. He picks up his phone and calls the writer to clarify the details of the event before making the decision of acceptance or rejection.

"Who's calling?" asks Mr. Loudon impolitely after he picks up the phone.

"It's George Goodwill from the community newspaper."

"From the Customs Office?" says Mr. Loudon who is hard on hearing. Click! Mr. Loudon quickly hangs up on him because he is very sensitive to strangers' calls, or rather, scammers' calls. In fact, prior to George's call, he had just received three from scammers who respectively pretended to be representatives from the border customs, the taxation agency, and DHL. He has mistaken the editor for another scammer.

George, who seldom calls business contacts more than once, makes an exception today. He immediately calls Mr. Loudon again. This time, he comes straight to the point when he hears Mr. Loudon's voice. "You sent a letter to the newspaper. I am the editor. I want to ask you a few questions about your legs, if you don't mind."

"Oh." Mr. Loudon seems to have heard him clearly this

time. "You are from the newspaper? Please speak loudly. My ears are not very good."

"Okay, I'll shout." George raises his voice. "I just want to clarify a few things with you."

"All right," says Mr. Loudon.

"Mr. Loudon," says George, "in your letter, you complain about your family doctor for the deteriorating condition of your legs. Do you mean to say it was he who caused your illness?"

"Please do not misunderstand me," says Mr. Loudon. "I do not mean that. I only complain that, about fifteen years ago, when I first discovered the trouble in my legs, he told me I had inherited it from my parents and I didn't have to worry about it."

"But you went back to him for annual checkups after that, didn't you?"

"Yes, I did. I had a checkup every year, or every other year."

"Since your condition got worse and worse, why didn't you raise the issue with him and request treatment?" asks George.

"Well," says Mr. Loudon hesitantly. "You must know that I am not a doctor. I just remembered what he told me before: it was from my parents, and it was a common thing that posed no danger. The illness developed slowly too. In the beginning, I only felt short periods of numbness in the legs, then it happened more often and lasted longer with each passing year. But I always remembered what he had told me, throughout the years. When it was really bad, I did tell him, and he would prescribe medications for me to control the swelling and reduce the pain. He never really did anything to cure it."

"But it is a well-known fact that there is no easy cure for edema, or leg swelling, as we often call it," says George.

"I know that," Mr. Loudon says in agreement. "But there are still things the doctor could do for a patient."

"What do you think he could have done for you?" George asks.

"I am not a doctor, and I don't know what he could have

done for me. But after twelve years of his treatment, my condition never improved. Instead, it got worse and worse, and walking became more and more difficult for me, until that lucky day three years ago when I had this opportunity to see an experienced doctor of Chinese medicine, a royal physician from Taiwan. He prescribed herbal medications for me for two years, which eliminated the trouble I had with my eyes and reduced half of the swelling in my legs, but the black lumps on my calves remained. Then, even this experienced Chinese doctor declared there was nothing else he could do for me and I just had to live with this now improved condition."

"Well," says George, "there is certainly no easy cure. Even the royal physician could not deliver the perfect results you had expected."

"I don't deny it is a very difficult condition to control or cure. In fact, three months after the herbal treatment, my legs started deteriorating again until I had many skin ulcers. Now I had these large black lumps on my calves. They did not look very pretty. And those runny skin ulcers never looked very pleasant. Worst of all, I could no longer walk as I used to. Every step was a struggle for me," sighs Mr. Loudon.

"Could you have other conditions elsewhere that might have caused your leg problems?" asks George.

"That's possible," says Mr. Loudon.

"Did you ever ask your family doctor to refer you to a specialist?" George asks.

"I had done so before," says Mr. Loudon, "but no treatment worked for me. That is why I continued to look for alternative treatment."

"Mr. Loudon," says George, "I am just curious why you seem to trust alternative medicine more than conventional medicine."

"It's not because I trust alternative medicine more. It is because conventional medicine just could not cure my illness. If it could, why would I spend my own money paying for alternative treatment?"

"I see," says George. "And in your letter you say you finally found Dr. Liu. How did you find him?"

"Before Christmas last year, a doctor friend told me, 'There is a competent acupuncturist in Toronto by the name of Wan Cheng Liu, who is an expert in treating different rare ailments.' Though I was skeptical, I went to see him after Christmas for a trial. I took two periods of treatment, twelve treatments per period, one treatment daily."

"Then what happened?" asks George.

"It was a miracle. The lumps on my calves shrank after each treatment, and so did the swelling. After Dr. Liu's acupuncture treatment, my overall condition improved tremendously. The purulent skin all dried up. I did not have difficulty in walking anymore. Actually, I could even run with ease. I became a totally new person. The great feeling is just beyond words!"

"I know you had your acupuncture treatment several months ago. And how are you doing now?" asks George.

"I am doing just great! I have been jogging ever since," says Mr. Loudon. "I owe a debt of gratitude to Dr. Liu. Without his help, I could have ended up having both legs amputated. Just imagine what my life would be without my legs!"

"I am impressed!" says George. "We will publish your letter in our newspaper so that more people can read your miraculous acupuncture treatment story."

Mr. Shawl's Heart

It was a windy Tuesday in the fall of 2018. Mrs. Shawl came to Dr. Liu's clinic for acupuncture treatment with her husband. Out of curiosity, her husband asked Dr. Liu for a free pulse test, if possible. Dr. Liu gladly offered him one. Within two minutes, Dr. Liu discovered that Mr. Shawl had a heart condition that required medical treatment, but Mr. Shawl disagreed.

"I just had my annual checkup last week, including an electrocardiogram. My family doctor told me everything was fine with me." Mr. Shawl did not believe he had any heart trouble, but he thanked Dr. Liu politely. He was confident that he needed no medical treatment.

"It's entirely up to you," said Dr. Liu. "But your condition will get worse."

On the third Sunday after his pulse test, Mr. Shawl went jogging before breakfast as usual. Nothing seemed out of the ordinary when he finished his daily exercise. He got back into the apartment building, went up to the elevator, and pushed the "Up" button. As soon as the elevator opened, he walked in and pushed the "4" button for the floor he lived on.

Bang! Bang!

Two loud noises were heard from the elevator, but no one knew what had happened inside.

A moment later, when his neighbor who was going to work was about to enter the elevator she had called for, she was shocked at seeing a motionless Mr. Shawl lying inside, blood gushing from his forehead. It looked like he had lost consciousness. The neighbor quickly ran to call Mrs. Shawl, who came running toward the elevator to see what had happened. Immediately she called 911 for assistance. Then she tried desperately to revive him by shaking him with all her might.

To her relief, Mr. Shawl regained consciousness five minutes after he passed out. The paramedics took him to the hospital, leaving a big puddle of blood inside the elevator that scared everyone who saw it. "What happened?' they all asked.

Mr. Shawl had exercised every morning. He never missed a day of jogging, not even in deep winter. His neighbors could not understand why this had happened to him.

"Did he have a heart attack?" his wife asked the doctor in the emergency room.

"We have just examined his heart," he told her. "The electrocardiogram shows his heart is fine. It doesn't indicate anything abnormal."

Mrs. Shawl breathed a sigh of relief. If he did not have a heart attack, he would still be a healthy man one way or another, she thought.

Mr. Shawl received seven stitches on his left forehead, stayed in the hospital for ten hours, during which he remained awake and active. He did not look like someone who had suffered a severe heart attack, or one who needed tender care. There was no reason to keep him in the overcrowded hospital, so late in the afternoon, the doctor in charge of his care declared him a healthy man who had temporarily fainted and whose injury on the forehead had been treated, and he was discharged from the hospital.

Mr. Shawl went home with his wife, feeling grateful he was still a healthy man. His wife felt consoled that he was still alive without a heart condition. She started thinking about how to improve his diet to enhance his health and quality of life.

Hearing about Mr. Shawl's accident, his friend Mrs. Watson came to visit him the following Saturday and found him feeble and pale, which she thought was an unmistakable sign of a weak heart. After receiving emergency treatment in the hospital and having taken his medications for ten days, Mr. Shawl was now so weak that he could hardly walk.

Mrs. Watson told him to seek help from Dr. Liu. His wife agreed with her, in fear he would suffer another attack of some type. Albeit reluctantly, Mr. Shawl finally accepted their advice, so his wife drove him to Dr. Liu's clinic that same afternoon.

Though Mr. Shawl did not believe in Dr. Liu wholeheartedly, by now he did suspect that he might really have a heart condition. He knew that he had few options available. That was why he had come to see him.

Mr. Shawl's condition improved after Dr. Lui's first acupuncture treatment. After twenty treatments, he looked like a healthy man again. His heart was strong, his energy level was high, his overall health improved significantly. Dr. Liu told him that he needed another period of twenty days to complete his treatment, but Mr. Shawl felt he was well enough and declined. His wife disagreed with him but could not change his mind. Again, it was a decision Mr. Shawl made by himself.

"I don't worry about my heart," Mr. Shawl told his wife after they left Dr. Liu's clinic. "I worry more about my blood pressure. If my blood pressure is too high, it can cause a fatal heart attack or a deadly stroke." But he did not know that in his course of treatment, Dr. Liu had also regulated his blood pressure, which had almost become normal and that, if he completed his treatment, he would not need medications to control it anymore.

Nonetheless, discontinuing Dr. Liu's acupuncture treatment did not mean Mr. Shawl neglected his own health. On the contrary, he always tried to take the best care of himself, including his heart. The following day he went to see his family doctor again, who recommended to him more than one type of medicine that could effectively control his blood pressure.

"Older is safer" was Mr. Shawl's belief. He told the doctor he liked the oldest medication for his condition.

"The oldest medicine is really effective," Mr. Shawl told Mrs. Watson excitedly after taking it for two days. "I can feel the difference. It's not only effective, but it's also inexpensive." Doubtless, twenty dollars' worth of the old medication would last more than ten days, and that was just about 20% of the cost of a single day's acupuncture treatment.

Nevertheless, older might not necessarily be safer or more effective, and less expensive might not really be better. The old medicine Mr. Shawl had chosen suppressed his heart so much that, one week later, he started complaining that his blood pressure just would not come down. Soon he found that his heart was in great distress, and his pain was so acute that he had to go to the hospital again.

This time, the cardiologist in the hospital found that his heart's valve leaflets were damaged and had to be replaced. If he had a mechanical valve replacement, he would have to take a blood thinner for the rest of his life. If he had a biological valve replacement, he would not need a blood thinner, but the valve would have to be replaced in ten years. One way or another, his medical procedure had to happen soon. Mr. Shawl made his choice and had his heart repaired without delay.

When Mr. Shawl woke up from his operation, he and his wife remained silent, each wondering, if he had listened to Dr. Liu, could he have saved his heart? Mr. Shawl thought the chance was fifty-fifty; Mrs. Shawl was even more convinced; but his friend Mrs. Watson was certain that Dr. Liu could have saved his heart if Mr. Shawl's acupuncture treatment had started on the day he had his pulse test, and if he had completed his treatment.

Now the only thing they all agreed on was that Dr. Liu could not help him anymore.

Your Pulse Says It All

Being an acupuncturist for fifty years, I have come across all kinds of patients. I do not remember most of those who came for treatment, then recovered and left, but I cannot forget a few who have done or said something out of the ordinary. One patient in his fifties named Howlie came to see me on a fall day three years ago. I had just given a free pulse test to Mr. Shawl, another middle-aged man. Howlie had brought along an advertisement, "Your Pulse Says It All," which I had placed in a health magazine. He said he was curious about how accurate my pulse tests could be, asking me if he could have a free trial. I said I would be delighted to offer him one.

"Do I need to stay for treatment after my pulse test?" he asked.

"No. Since it is a free pulse test, you have no obligation to stay for any treatment, even if you have a condition," I answered.

He nodded. "When can I do it?"

"Right now," I said, signaling him to sit on the seat in front of me at the diagnosis desk.

He sat down and put his wrist on the wrist cushion. Then, I placed three of my fingers on his pulse, applying different degrees of pressure on each. In less than two minutes, I told him what I had discovered.

"You have some problems with your heart," I said. "More specifically, your heart is weak, you have palpitations, and you suffer occasional heart pain." He had the same condition I had found with Mr. Shawl, who had just left my clinic.

"No. You are wrong," said he. "I don't have any trouble with my heart. My last annual electrocardiogram showed that my heart was perfectly healthy." He nearly repeated the same words Mr. Shawl had told me when Mr. Shawl was informed of his condition.

"But your heart is not perfectly healthy," I said. "That is my diagnosis. You need treatment to improve the condition. But of course, any treatment decision is up to you to make."

"Thanks anyway, but I don't think I need any treatment for now."

The unconvinced visitor left, and I went on with my work, forgetting about him in no time.

Exactly one week later, at about 9:00 a.m., my phone rang. I picked it up and heard Howlie's voice.

"Sir, do you still remember me?" He did not sound very friendly. I was surprised it was him, wondering if he had changed his mind and had decided to seek treatment.

"Yes, I do. You came to my clinic and had a free pulse test last week," I said. "What can I do for you?"

"I don't want you to do anything more for me. You have done enough for me already," he said coldly. "Last week, before I saw you, I had no trouble with my heart, but after you touched my pulse, you said I had some heart trouble. And now I really have all the trouble you told me I had! How would you explain that to me?"

"What do you mean?" I said.

"Before I saw you last week, I was a healthy man. After I saw you, I became an unhealthy man."

"That was what I told you last week, but you just didn't believe me," I said.

"What do you think I should I do now?" he asked.

"Come for treatment. Then you shall be fine."

"So, that is how you do business!" He became very rude now. "You touched my pulse, planted all the trouble in me, and now you will have my business!"

What an outrageous accusation he was making! It was an insult to me that could ruin my reputation and soil my character. It looked like he was going to sue me. What a joke it would be if I really had to go to court to prove that I did not plant any illness in him by touching his pulse!

I knew there was no chance he could win such a lawsuit, but just think of the time and the legal fees any lawsuit would cost! Regardless of its merit, if such a bizarre case was reported in the media, it would not do me any good. I tried to calm him down to prevent him from escalating the case.

"Gentleman, I want to repeat to you once more that I did not give you your heart trouble. You already had the condition before you came to my clinic last week. I only gave you a pulse test, and then I just reported the results of the test to you. I told you your heart needed treatment, but you declined and left. Please don't accuse me of starting the heart trouble for you. I am not God. I don't have the ability to give any person any ailments by touching their wrist. Your heart disease is not transmittable; it's not contagious. No one could have passed it to you; nor can you pass it to anyone else. You can go to your other doctors and ask them if any doctor could have possibly planted your heart disease in you."

He became silent for a while, and then said. "What should I do then?"

"As I told you just now," I said, "come and I will give you acupuncture treatment. Then you will be fine."

To my surprise, he listened to me this time. Forty minutes later, he arrived at my clinic, looking pale and tired. Fortunately, he started his treatment without further delay. After his first treatment, he said that he felt much more energetic. Then, he continued to come until he finished his course of fifteen treatments, during which his conditions kept improving until all his symptoms disappeared. He smiled throughout his last day of treatment. I could see he was satisfied with the treatment results.

"Do I need to come back for more treatment?" he asked me on the fifteenth day.

"No," I said, "unless your ailments recur, which is unlikely, at least, within this year." Then he disappeared like most of my other patients who had recovered from their illness.

Thank God, I thought. I had finally turned a grumpy, pale man into a happy man of ruddy complexion and had probably avoided a lawsuit. But to be fair, he had done no harm to me or my career, though he is one of the patients I can never forget. Personal grievances aside, I find him a lovely person who enriches my memory. I respect and love him as I do my other patients.

Probably you may wonder what could have happened to Howlie if he had refused treatment. Based on my fifty years' experience, without proper treatment, his heart condition would deteriorate until a heart attack struck him. That was what happened to my other patient, Mr. Shawl, who first declined treatment, then opted for incomplete treatment only after he suffered his first heart attack, which then resulted in his second attack, and after that, I could not treat him anymore.

37 Years Vs. 30 Days

A grateful Jeanie Chanson unwraps her gift before Dr. Liu in his clinic, looking very proud.

"I have a gift for you, Dr. Liu," she says as she presents it to him. "I spent three months embroidering it stitch by stitch."

It is an embroidered golden portrait of Bodhisattva, 70 cm wide by 120 cm high with the following lines at the bottom:

Role-model doctor with the highest morals,
Best acupuncturist of all mortals.

"I can't take it," says Dr. Liu. "You can sell it for five thousand dollars, at least."

"Why sell it? It's not for sale!" she says, displeased. "It is for you! You have saved my life."

"You are shortening my life when you say this," says the humble doctor, who just cannot find a good reason to refuse the gift. "Your illness was not big deal, anyway."

"No big deal?" Jeanie protests. "You just didn't suffer it yourself! Thirty-seven years, dear Dr. Liu! Thirty-seven years of pain and suffering. Thirty-seven years of bedridden life! And you said it was no big deal!" She wants to cry.

Just half a year ago, Jeanie was a different person.

At the age of 68, the bedridden Jeanie Chanson had decided not to seek any more treatment for her multiple ailments. She had too many ailments and too many painful experiences to list. Jeanie suffered from chronic pain in her neck, shoulders, arms, legs, spine, knees, all the joints in her body, and all her nerves and muscles.

Her pain was not the familiar type that most seniors of her

age suffered. It was so acute that she could not sleep throughout the night. She could not turn her body in bed. She could not put on her socks and shoes. She could not stand and move her feet. Her arms, legs, back, and her entire body always felt stiff with sore. When she tried to raise her arms, she felt they would break. When she tried to raise her legs, she felt they were as heavy as lead, and if she forced them, they would snap. If she tried to bend down, the pain could instantly make her faint. To reduce her suffering, she always lay in bed and tried to avoid movement. That was Jeanie's life.

Her painful life started thirty-seven years earlier, after she gave birth to her daughter, Betty. That windy wintry morning, she suddenly found herself in labor soon after her husband had gone to work. Her neighbors immediately called a tricycle taxi to send her to the hospital. As soon as Mr. Chanson heard about it, he rushed to the hospital to look after her.

Jeanie was thirty-one, and the obstetrician asked if she wanted to have a C-section birth, but she declined, opting for a natural birth. The obstetrician told her it was not a problem, since mother and baby both appeared to be very healthy. Jeanie was in labor for thirty-three hours, and a lovely baby girl of eight pounds was finally delivered the following evening, but she kept shivering after the baby was born, which became her cause of worry.

The delivery room was chilly, perhaps around eighteen degrees Celsius. Jeanie had never thought she would need an additional blanket in the hospital, and she had not brought one. Neither did she ask for one from the hospital, for she thought the baby would be born at any moment, and then they could return home, but the delivery took a day and a half, during which time she was cold and hungry. Unavoidably, she also lost much blood during delivery. She became a much weaker person when she finally returned home with her bundle of joy.

When Jeanie started breastfeeding her baby on the fourth day, her originally faint pain turned acute. She thought it was probably normal, especially for mothers who had a 33-hour delivery, but her case was not quite the same. Her pain persisted. She not only felt it in the first few days, but also the following week, and through the first month, then the second... But the thrilling joy of motherhood helped her survive the pain.

Nonetheless, when her pain did not disappear after three months, Mr. Chanson became worried and took her back to the obstetrician who suspected that she might have lost too much blood and had an iron-deficiency condition. Therefore, he prescribed iron supplements for her, among other medications, including painkillers, in case she needed them. But after she had taken the medications, her condition did not improve; instead, it deteriorated. Breastfeeding the baby became a more formidable challenge for her.

The following month, Jeanie went to see another reputed physician in the hospital specializing in women's diseases, who prescribed antibiotics and again pain-relievers, among other medications. Jeanie took the new medications for three weeks as instructed, but still in vain.

It was through pain and effort that she breastfed the baby until she was seven months old. Though she loved holding her in her arms, she had never been able to because of the pain all over her body. Then, she weaned her and let her husband feed her grain food instead.

But what had happened was just a prelude to Jeanie's battle against her pain. After failing to find a cure at the local hospital, she started seeing the best osteopathic doctors of Western medicine elsewhere and of traditional Chinese medicine, including acupuncturists and massage therapists. She went to the well-known Capital Hospital where she saw the best pain specialist who was trained in one of the most prestigious medical schools in America. He gave her a comprehensive examination including a urine test, a blood test that included numerous test items she did not understand, and an expensive CT scan of her brain, heart, lungs, liver, spleen, and kidneys. To her disappointment, the costly diagnostic tests failed to identify the cause of her illness. The reputed physician only prescribed two types of pain relievers for her without telling her what medications she was going to take. He asked her to come back three months later should her pain persist.

Unsurprisingly, her pain remained acute after she had taken the medications for four weeks, and her condition had deteriorated further. She felt that her pain was so bad that she could not even wait for another week, let alone two more months.

Life was just unfriendly to Jeanie. The next week, she had trouble with her bowel movements. She had failed to empty her bowel for seven days, which finally resulted in severe anal bleeding and swelling, sending her to the neighboring city's Hospital for Women and Children for emergency treatment. She was in great distress until her constipation problem was resolved. Only after a sudden deliverance, did she finally groan with relief, wondering why she had more health problems than other people.

During her hospitalization, she complained to her physician about the acute pain all over her body, which had caused her constipation. The doctor then ordered for her an NMR test to analyze various chemical elements in her body that might reveal the root of her ailments. It was a test that cost half her husband's annual income, but again, no definite cause related to her pain and other health issues was found. Jeanie and her husband were deeply disappointed beyond words. Dropping the newly prescribed medications into her handbag, again Jeanie left the hospital in dejection, swallowing her tears without uttering a word.

The newly prescribed tablets she had received were not much different from what she had taken previously. They were similar in size, shape, and weight. "Am I going to depend on painkillers my entire life?" she wondered after checking the medication label.

Mr. Chanson grew even more anxious and became more restless after Jeanie's hospitalization also failed to cure her pain. How could there be such an illness that so many reputed doctors could not even identify, let alone cure? Both husband and wife had lost confidence in the entire healthcare system, especially contemporary medicine.

By now they had used up their $200,000 savings, which was originally intended as the down payment for a new home and for Betty's education. From now on, any treatment would mean debt for them.

"I'm not going to see any more doctors," Jeanie said sadly.

"Please don't say that," Mr. Chanson said. "I am sure we will find the right doctor before long. Betty needs you. She needs a healthy mom." Tears welled up in her eyes again when she heard her daughter's name.

"Jeanie," Mr. Chanson continued, "in fact, I have just found a herbalist in the City of Seacoast. It is just a two-hour flight. He uses no other medicine except fresh herbs. It is 100% organic, all natural, or wild plants only. I hear his herbal treatments are very effective."

"I'd rather not try yet," she said.

"Jeanie, delaying does not help. The earlier you try, the easier it is to cure." He looked at her lovingly.

Refusing his offer would disappoint him. "But how can we get back on the same day?" she said reluctantly, somehow feeling hope burning in her again.

Betty was now a toddler. How Jeanie wished she could quickly get back on her feet and hold her in her arms! How she wished she could play with her, walk with her, and run after her! How she wished the herbalist could cure her pain once and for all!

"We will pay the herbalist a flat fee and stay in his thatched hut until you complete a course of treatment," Mr. Chanson said excitedly. "It's a clean place, free of pollution, unlike the cities."

The following Saturday, Jeanie's parents came over to take care of Betty. She and her husband flew to Seacoast. From the airport they hired a taxi that took them to the herbalist's residence in the mountain village fifty kilometers away.

The thatched hut was much more comfortable than they had expected. It was bright and clean with a double bed and all the basic furniture they needed. The best part of the package was that they could cook their own meals.

Most impressively, they could pick vegetables directly from the many vegetable beds surrounding the hut. There were celeries, tomatoes, cucumbers, broccoli, cauliflowers, and many more, half of which they had never seen in the city. They could also pick their own fruits from the trees, such as apples, oranges, starfruits, plums, lychee, and longan, among others that they did not even know.

It was a cool, breezy place in summer. They could hear cocks crowing at daybreak, cicadas singing at noon, and frogs croaking at night. To add to their delight, there was a fish pond teeming with carps, crabs, shrimps, and other fish. They could conveniently catch any they liked, using a huge net with a long handle. If they wanted fresh poultry, they could just let the herbalist know three hours ahead of time and they would have everything they wanted. All these were included in the fee of $20,000 that covered Jeanie's entire medical treatment.

"You can't find a better place than this," said Mr. Chanson. Jeanie nodded, but she was just cautiously positive. She would rather wait for her treatment results than jump to any premature judgment. Beautiful though it was, Jeanie found the place rather damp, which was normal in the mountain village in summer when it rained more often. Strangely, she felt her body did not like it, but she did not complain. She was hoping against hope that the herbalist could cure her illness. "This is my last try!" she said to herself. "I won't try any more if I fail this time."

Besides enjoying the beautiful sunshine, clean air, clear

mountain spring water, and the fresh food Mr. Chanson cooked for her, Jeanie took three glasses of fresh herbal juice prepared by the herbalist daily: one before breakfast; one at noon; and the third, one hour before going to bed. She felt refreshed whenever she drank it. The general feeling was positive.

Jeanie's mood lifted, and she even smiled once or twice a day. It cheered up Mr. Chanson, who felt that every penny spent on the trip was worth it. Jeanie remained hopeful in the first week when she felt as if her pain was starting to ease. Her muscles were not as tense and her elbows and knees felt a little better, but then everything just stayed the same. She felt no further improvement in the second week or the third.

Undeniably, she did feel healthier when her herbal treatment ended, but the improvement was just a feeling attributed to the new environment and the organic food and fruit, which had not significantly eased the pain anywhere on her body. In fact, all her pain remained nearly as bad as it had been when she came.

"It's a good treat, but not a cure," she sighed.

Her husband looked gloomy again. "Gosh! What are we to do now?" he said to himself. Jeanie tried to look cheerful to cheer him up. They left the picturesque village and returned home.

After that, Jeanie would see herbal practitioners only when she really had to, who would then prescribe ten or twenty packages of herbal medications for her. Each visit would cost twenty or thirty dollars. Though it was still expensive for her husband, who was the only breadwinner in the family, they could still afford it—he just had to prioritize the expenditure of his income by saving on food and other necessities.

In the following thirty-some years, she could not remember how many packages of Chinese herbal medications and how many doses of Western medicine, especially painkillers, she had taken. She was just sure that she must have taken at least 3000 packages of herbal medications and far more than

20,000 painkillers, which thankfully had not killed her. Despite her resistance, Mr. Chanson had taken her to at least thirty more doctors throughout the years. She was hospitalized twice more, once due to her fainting and once due to her head injury, both triggered by severe pain.

Jeanie always felt guilty because she was unable to look after Betty, who kept growing by herself, just like a small wild tree in the Seacoast village she had visited. She saw her crawling when she was eight months old, then learning to stand on her feet, then walking, then running. Then, she saw her going to school by herself, carrying a tiny school bag on her back. She kept dreaming of finding a quick cure for her pain so that she could walk Betty to school, hand in hand. Though each painful day seemed as long as a year for her, she still found time flying when she saw her daughter finishing kindergarten, then elementary school, then middle school, and then turning into an adult in the year she graduated from high school. How agonizing Betty's childhood and teenage years had been for Jeanie! And how happy she was that Betty had become a mature young adult!

What moved Jeanie to tears was that her "motherless" daughter had earned the highest overall score on the college entrance examination among the one million high school graduates in the province. Betty was accepted by the University of Toronto, which offered her a full scholarship.

After telling her parents about the university's offer, Betty became hesitant, not knowing what to do. Ever since the age of six she had been feeling guilty herself, thinking that it was her birth that had made her mother so ill. She could not sleep a wink that night, but strangely she had the premonition that she would someday find a cure for her mother if she went to the university. Yet, she hated to leave her parents because her mother needed her.

"Why are your eyes red, my child?" her mother asked her the next morning. "You should be proud of yourself for being accepted by U of T. Numerous students dream of going there but never have a chance. It is such a great opportunity for you." Her mother's words were so soft, soothing, and warm.

"I cannot take it, Mom," Betty choked. "I want to stay and take care of you."

"Silly girl, how can you really take care of me?" Jeanie said. "As you know, Mom has been to all the best hospitals far and near. I have seen all the best doctors of conventional medicine and the best alternative practitioners, including herbalists, acupuncturists, and massage therapists. I have taken more medicine than the food you have eaten your whole life. And you know our family is basically broke because of my health problems. If the best hospitals and all those best doctors cannot do anything for me, what can you really do for me even if you stay?

"Mom—" she cried.

"If you really love me and want to take care of me, the only way is accepting the offer; study hard and find a well-paying job. Then, help me find a doctor in Toronto who can cure my pain," Jeanie said, wiping the tears from Betty's face with her forehead, as Betty bent down to hug her.

"But—" Betty wanted to say something, but her mother cut her short.

"Look, my child," said Jeanie. "If you go to U of T, someday you may really find a cure for me in Toronto. It's a city full of talented people. And that is the only possibility, and perhaps the only chance you may have. I am still young and can manage everything myself when you are away. Listen to Mom, and you will be happy one day."

Betty's eyes brightened at hearing the idea of finding a cure for her mother in Toronto. Still in each other's arms, mother and daughter were drowned in tears.

Seven years later, Betty, who had not only completed her BA at U of T but also her MBA, had opened a private high school for international students. She had settled in Toronto and married a doctor trained at the University of Toronto. When they were financially secure, they invited her parents to live with them, and they accepted. In the year of their reunion, Betty was thirty-five and Jeanie was sixty-six. For the first time, Betty was confident her mother's illness would be cured before long.

She and her husband found for her mother the best pain specialists of Western medicine as well as the best TCM practitioners in Toronto, including the best ones from Taiwan, Hong Kong, and mainland China. Nonetheless, though they were the best and though each did their best for her mother, after two years of extensive treatment, none of them was able to cure her chronic pain. How disappointed everyone felt!

But Betty was just as stubborn as her father when searching for doctors for her mother. All over again, she collected all the news reports available about the best Canadian pain specialists of conventional medicine, Chinese herbal practitioners, and acupuncturists, not only by looking at their own advertisements but also by carefully reading and analyzing, one by one, the news stories about them and their patients' testimonials.

At long last, on her mother's 68th birthday, their decades-long search was about to end. It was God's will that this loving daughter had found an acupuncturist by the name of Wan Cheng Liu, who had a PhD in acupuncture. His clinic was in the medical building opposite her private school on Victoria Park Avenue.

As soon as she became sure that Dr. Liu was the doctor she was looking for, she called her husband, who also agreed. Then, she immediately walked over to Dr. Liu's clinic to make an appointment with him in person. Her feeling was good after meeting him. On the same afternoon, her mother, who had not been able to walk for thirty-seven years, came to see him, supported by Betty and her father on both sides.

No one dared to expect too much from Dr. Liu on the first

day. After all, Jeanie had seen tens, if not hundreds, of doctors, including acupuncturists, during the past thirty-seven years, and none had ever significantly eased her pain. Her husband had brought along a heavy bag of at least 500 lab reports she had collected during the past decades. They wanted to show them to Dr. Liu, lest he misdiagnose his patient.

To their surprise, Dr. Liu did not even bother to look at any one of them. Instead, he gave Jeanie a pulse test, which took only about two or three minutes. Then, he confidently told them that the patient's illness was curable. Jeanie felt hope starting to burn in her again. It was an indescribable feeling she had missed for more than thirty years.

Dr. Liu asked Jeanie to lie on the acupuncture bed, but she had too much pain to walk into the acupuncture room, so Mr. Chanson and Betty helped her, literally carrying her up there. She had too much pain to take off her shoes and socks, so they did both for her. She had too much pain to remove her shirt, so they did it for her too. Betty stood in the corner, just in case she would be needed for emergency assistance, while her father stayed outside.

A moment later, Dr. Liu came to give Jeanie the first treatment. He flicked the needles into her acupoints, covered her with two small blankets, and then left her to sleep. Approximately fifty minutes later, Dr. Liu came back into the acupuncture room and said, "Did you fall asleep?" It was the standard question he would ask to wake up his patient when the treatment was over.

"Yes, I did," Jeanie said.

"Try to get up and see how you feel," said Dr. Liu, with Betty standing by, joined by her anxious father who had been standing outside the door.

Jeanie raised her legs and was astonished that she could bend them. After only one treatment!

Betty and her father were stupefied, with their mouths and eyes wide open, not knowing what to say.

One treatment and Jeanie was able to bend her knees! It was something she had not been able to do for more than thirty years.

"Miraculous! Miraculous! Just miraculous!" Betty kept screaming, unable to hold back her happy tears. At this moment, fixing her eyes on her now senior mother, Betty realized that her mother had been right to encourage her to come to study at the University of Toronto. If she had not accepted U of T's offer, she would not have come to Toronto. If she had not come to Toronto, she would not have found Dr. Liu. And without Dr. Liu's treatment, her mother would continue to suffer her unbearable pain throughout her life.

Even before Jeanie had completed her treatment, they were all positive that she would be cured. The whole family left Dr. Liu in disbelief, crying grateful, happy tears. No one could talk in a normal voice, so they all remained silent, looking away from each other to hide their tearful eyes.

The next day, Jeanie came back to Dr. Liu for her second treatment, more confident than the previous day, as her condition kept improving. She continued with her subsequent treatments until she completed two courses, or a total of thirty treatments. All her pain had disappeared, though it was not a 100% complete recovery. After all, she had been bedridden for thirty-some years, which had caused certain issues in her bone structure and elsewhere that needed some time for re-adjustment. But Jeanie was able to walk swiftly and live a normal life. She could bend down and move her neck, arms, and legs freely without any discomfort. Her entire body, including her spine and all her joints, was now pain-free.

Jeanie felt she had become a new person. When her 30th treatment was completed, Dr. Liu declared she had been cured. He told her that she had suffered from the *bi* syndrome that included three symptoms: *feng* (wind), *han* (cold), and *shi* (dampness). "No more treatments are necessary," he said. "Just take care of yourself and, gradually, you will have your complete recovery."

"Miracle! Miracle! Great miracle!" No words could describe Jeanie's joy. Dr. Liu's 30-day acupuncture treatment had cured 37 years of unendurable pain!

You Are Shortening My Life*

Everyone on Poultry Lane knew that Shawn, a 68-year-old retired factory worker, had a severe stroke in August. He was taken to emergency and was hospitalized for nine days. Then, he left the hospital before his treatment was completed because he had used up all his money, including his savings and whatever he had borrowed from friends and neighbors. He and his wife were a childless couple with no one else to look to for help. Though it was a risk, his 69-year-old wife took him home anyway. That same night, Shawn suffered a second stroke, dealing his wife another blow.

Shawn became totally disabled after the second stroke and had to depend on his wife for everything. He had pain and numbness all over his body and was too weak to lift a cup of water, let alone feed himself and go to the toilet. Equally dreadful, he had a stiff tongue that could not move, and so he could no longer speak. The hospital was the only place that could cure him, but sending him back there would require a new deposit that would cost ten years of the couple's pensions, which they just could not afford.

---

*The content of this story, much of which first appeared in various Chinese publications more than thirty years ago, comes from an informal interview the author conducted with Dr. Liu on June 21, 2022. Dr. Liu's opinion is that it is old stuff, not worth writing about. The author, however, thinks this story is a glimpse at the earlier career of a benevolent doctor, and its inclusion therefore makes this collection more complete. Like those in the other stories, all the patients' names in this story have been changed to protect their privacy.

The following day, Shawn's wife begged the community health center to set up a home acupuncture treatment bed for her husband. Finally, the health center agreed after she paid a fee that ate up a whole month's pension. Additional charges would apply based on the acupuncturist's visits. The acupuncturist from the health center told her that Shawn would recover after three courses of treatment, but before he completed the first course, the acupuncturist mysteriously disappeared, probably because he had found the patient too difficult to cure. Shawn's wife was left scrambling for help again. Finally, she decided to take him to the city's hospital for outpatient treatment instead.

It was with great effort that Shawn managed to lean on his wife's shoulders, and it was with the support of his wife and a cane that he made it into a tricycle taxi that took him to the city's hospital. A trip that would take a healthy person twenty minutes took Shawn two hours. Then, the return trip would take the same time, or even more.

Seeing the loving old couple suffering in every aspect of their life, the nurses in the acupuncture department of the hospital felt sorry for them, talking about them during their lunch break. Wan Cheng Liu, a PhD candidate in acupuncture, already a licensed medical doctor, known as "Miracle Acupuncturist" throughout the province, was doing his residency in the hospital. When he heard about Shawn's crisis, he put down his lunch and went to the outpatient area to see what the old couple looked like. Near the exit, he saw them struggling to leave the hospital, inch by inch. One could imagine what a pain it was for a feeble 69-year-old lady to take out of the hospital her paralyzed husband who was taller and heavier than her. Dr. Liu did not know the exact details and he dared not ask, but he found their sufferings indescribable, simply beyond human dignity.

His eyes blurring, he walked up to them and said, "I will go to your home to give you acupuncture treatment tomorrow, so you don't need to come."

Shawn and his wife looked at this young doctor in disbelief. Shawn's wife gave him their address and cried, "How can we ever thank you enough!" They wanted to kowtow to him, but they could not, because Shawn could not move, and neither could his wife who was holding his weight with both hands and her shoulders.

"I'll see you at your home late in the afternoon tomorrow," said Dr. Liu. Late afternoon was the only time he could work out for Shawn. During the regular hours, he had to study and treat other patients admitted by the hospital.

Shawn's home was a small bachelor's apartment that was occupied by a double bed, a wardrobe, a shabby dresser, a small table, and two old wooden chairs. There was so little room left that Dr. Liu could not even move freely while giving the patient treatment. Dr. Liu's first treatment at once eased Shawn's pain and numbness. After that he came at the same hour every day for twenty-nine more days, until Shawn regained his speech ability and could walk swiftly without pain or numbness. Dr. Liu's benevolence moved Shawn and his wife to tears.

Dr. Liu declined payments and gifts from the old couple, but on his last trip, when he was about to leave them, the old couple insisted, "If you don't even eat a few of the dumplings we have made for you, we will kneel in front of you until you do." When patients knelt, it always scared Dr. Liu. He just could not accept it or even allow it. He knew that people could kneel before God. In ancient times the populace would kneel before the kings and emperors. In present times, some juniors may also kneel before the deceased in the coffin. Kneeling itself carries so much meaning. In any case, he just would not let patients kneel before him. Dr. Liu felt he had no choice but to accept their offer. Thus, he ate a bowl of the dumplings they had made for him, instantly cheering up the grateful old couple.

News about Shawn's recovery spread throughout the community, and soon everybody heard about the benevolent

Dr. Liu. The former head of the community center, who had been suffering from chronic back pain and a hunchback, was among the first patients to seek free acupuncture treatment from Dr. Liu, who gave her one session on the day he accepted her, and her pain was gone. After two more treatments, she was pain-free, walking swiftly with a straight back. Because everybody knew her, especially her chronic back pain and hunchback, she became an effective advertisement for Dr. Liu.

Within the next few days, patients swarmed to her home, begging her assistance to ask for free treatments from Dr. Liu. The 50-year-old lady living half a street away had a painful back that bent down 90 degrees. She could not walk steadily even with a cane. To her, crawling would be safer than walking.

"When the pain is bad, I just want to hang myself!" she told a close friend.

But she was also a lucky one. Dr. Liu just gave her one treatment, and she was able to walk with a straight back.

"I really wanted to kneel down before him when he came again the next day!" she told her neighbors afterward, but Mr. Liu never knew what she was thinking and what she had said.

You can imagine how busy Dr. Liu became after this. To cut the story short, during his three-year PhD candidacy, he provided free acupuncture treatment to more than 300 patients who had suffered various diseases, all during after-work hours or on the weekend. Due to the extra work, he seldom slept more than six hours a day himself.

"There comes the Living Buddha!" Residents of Poultry Lane would quickly line along both sides of the narrow street when they heard that Dr. Liu was coming. Poorly educated patients, whose vocabulary was not very large, sincerely called him "Living Buddha" and "Living Deity," but Dr. Liu would feel offended when he heard these nicknames and stop them rudely, "You are shortening my life when you say this!" Only then would they switch to the common title "Doctor." All the patients knew that Dr. Liu had great compassion for the underprivileged. Providing them with free medical treatment was his way of showing his love for them and respect for human dignity. He enjoyed doing it and he did it tirelessly. He was already a role model for his peers in the early years of his career.

Albeit undereducated, Dr. Liu's patients were quick learners. To show their sincere respect for him, before him they would call him "Dr. Liu," but behind him they would still call him "Living Buddha," "Living Deity," "Needle God," "No. 1 Needle," and "Miracle Acupuncturist." They just felt that "Doctor" was too common and it lowered him to an unacceptable level, and that only the nicknames more accurately described who their doctor was.

About the Miracle Acupuncturist

Ladies and gentlemen, thank you for attending my video conference today. As you all know, this conference is intended to answer questions related to Dr. Wan Cheng Liu, the "Miracle Acupuncturist." I am much honored to have this opportunity to share with you my limited knowledge about him.

I have received a list of questions here, which I will answer one by one. Please feel free to interrupt me if you need clarification at any time.

The first question is, "Is Dr. Liu a fictitious figure invented by the author?"

The answer is no. Dr. Wan Cheng Liu is first and foremost a doctor, an acupuncturist who lives in Ontario, Canada. He eats food and lives under a roof. You are assured that he is a "real" doctor whose clinic is on Victoria Park Avenue, north of Finch Avenue East, in Toronto.

The second question is, "Did the writer Harry J. Huang invent the title 'Miracle Acupuncturist' for Dr. Liu?"

No. Dr. Liu's "title," "Miracle Acupuncturist," or "Miracle Doctor," and other synonymous nicknames can be traced back to the 1980s. They come from newspapers, magazines, books, and patients' testimonials posted online. The title "Miracle Acupuncturist," among others, has been given to him by his patients of the past forty years from different cities in the world. It has nothing to do with the author.

Following are stories from three of the numerous patients who have given him the nickname, or synonymous "titles."

On July 19, 1986, when he was a medical doctor in China,

he was called to treat a prominent visiting businessman who had an asymmetrically functioning *yin-yang* face. For years, when the right side of the patient's face sweated, his left side would remain dry. He had sought treatment from various reputed specialists, but in vain. When Dr. Liu arrived in his hotel room, the patient's right face was covered with sweat while the left was dry. Dr. Liu flicked a needle into his *taiyang* acupoint. Then, he manipulated the needle up and down and from side to side. In about five minutes, the patient felt fine sweat beads oozing from the pores of his left face. In a fit of delight, he sprang to his feet, seized Dr. Liu's arms, and shouted out, "Needle God! Needle God!" "Needle" in this context means "acupuncture." Literally, it means "Acupuncture God." That was when and how Dr. Liu's nickname "Needle God," or "Acupuncture God," came into being.

Then came a television reporter, Ms. Yale, from JSTV who wanted to witness how miraculous Dr. Liu's acupuncture treatment was. She asked Dr. Liu to treat her senior colleague's paralyzed daughter. In the last months of the woman's pregnancy, one of her legs became paralyzed, and after she gave birth to her baby, which was a long and difficult delivery, she became paralyzed and could not even get off the bed. Ms. Yale thought any miracle should require eight to ten treatments at least, if not months. While they waited in the living room, Dr. Liu started treating the patient in her bedroom. To the reporter's disbelief, hardly had they sipped the tea served by the host when they saw the patient, who had been lying in bed for more than a month, walking out of her bedroom all by herself. She even picked up her baby and held her in her arms, which she had not been able to do due to her paralysis.

What a miracle it was! Everyone present was astounded beyond words, simply bursting into an applause to show their respect and gratitude for Dr. Liu. "Needle God! Needle God, indeed!" they cried.

The third patient, Mr. Ford of Toronto, has a different

story. After he injured his back at work on January 3, eighteen years ago, he could not sit, stand, or sleep, let alone walk. He could only lie in bed, and even in bed, he dared not move, for his shoulders, chest, and back would hurt unbearably if he did. Putting on a shirt or a hat, speaking, coughing, and even breathing would cause him unendurable pain. The physician took X-rays of his injured back and prescribed the strongest painkillers for him to relieve his pain. He then reported his injury to the Workplace Safety and Insurance Board (WSIB). However, the painkillers neither improved Mr. Ford's conditions nor relieved his pain. Each time he walked to the washroom, he had to lean on his wife's shoulders, dragging his feet forward inch by inch.

By chance he found Dr. Liu and sought treatment from him. Unable to walk unassisted, he came to see him with a cane, supported by his wife. "After the first acupuncture treatment, I felt so much better," he said. "After the second treatment, I threw away my cane. After several more treatments I fully recovered."

He asked Dr. Liu if he could lift heavy things again, and the answer was yes. Beyond his understanding, after he had gone back to work for quite some time, he received a letter from WSIB stating that they had assessed his injury and concluded that he had become totally disabled and was eligible for total-disability benefits. Ford, who did not want to collect disability benefits, was grateful he had recovered from his injury. He called Dr. Liu a miracle acupuncturist who delivered unbelievable results. In the patient Jane Nash's words, "Dr. Liu is the only doctor in the world that can deliver these miraculous results."

These are just a few of the numerous patients who have called Dr. Liu "Miracle Acupuncturist," "Miracle Doctor," and "Needle God." I should have called him "Miracle Doctor," but for various reasons, I chose *Miracle Acupuncturist* for the book title instead.

The next question is, "There are so many doctors and acupuncturists in Canada and the rest of the world, what makes Dr. Liu different from his peers?"

That's a good question. My guess is that Dr. Liu is not only a knowledgeable doctor and a scholar who is full of ideas and an outstanding inventor of treatment methods, but he treats his patients with his heart and soul, in his own words. After earning his three degrees, a BA (1976), an MA (1984), and a PhD (1990), all in traditional Chinese medicine and including acupuncture, he continued to invent or improve treatment techniques and skills, in addition to conducting studies and writing books and articles. Dr. Liu is the creator of the Amur Acupuncture Theory. The flick-insertion acu-treatment technique he invented has been popularly used by fellow acupuncturists worldwide. It not only reduces the patient's pain when the needle goes into the acupoint, but it has unknown positive treatment effects that remain to be studied.

As is well known, Dr. Liu is not only a scholar and a professor of acupuncture, but he is a role model with the highest ethical standards for young acupuncturists and is a one-man hospital who effectively treats more than 100 rare and difficult diseases, many of which are considered impossible to cure by conventional doctors. There are not that many doctors and acupuncturists in their seventies in North America and elsewhere who can effectively treat more than 100 difficult diseases and who work tirelessly for the patients seven days a week.

An additional point I wish to share with you is that Dr. Liu is a humble scholar who does not claim superiority in knowledge, treatment skills, treatment results, or treatment success rates. As a scholar, he knows every doctor, including himself, has his or her own strengths and weaknesses because they are all humans. Dr. Liu's patients, on the other hand, love calling him Needle God, Acupuncture God, Living Buddha, Living Deity and the like because of his benevolence and other godly characteristics, besides his outstanding treatment skills, but Dr. Liu never compares himself with any other medical workers and he feels offended by any nickname containing "God," "Buddha," or "Deity." All he does every day, seven days a week, is focus on treating every patient who comes to see him in his clinic. He treats them holistically, with his heart and soul, trying to cure their illnesses within the shortest time he can. Perhaps these are what makes him different from other doctors and acupuncturists.

Any other questions?

I see you are all shaking your heads. I know my answers to the questions were very brief, but I would still like to conclude our video conference, as scheduled. I hope you agree that Dr. Liu deserves the nickname "Miracle Acupuncturist."

Finally, thank you for lending me your time and patience, and I wish everyone good health and longevity.

Appendix

Why I Accepted SARS and Covid-19 Patients

"Dr. Liu, the SARS virus and COVID-19 virus are both very contagious. You were aware that you could easily catch them, but without hesitation you accepted SARS and COVID-19 patients and treated them in your clinic that has no protective equipment like the hospital wards. Why didn't you reject them?"

"It is my firm belief that a doctor's job is saving patients' lives. If one has to die, the doctor should die first. It is not just a slogan that many student doctors are learning from their textbooks. This is part of my medical ethics.

"Every profession has its own ethics. I clearly remember a case during the tsunami in Japan. A female broadcaster was warning and asking the residents to flee as the tsunami was surging toward them, including herself. She kept saying, "Run! Run! Run! Everybody, run..." until she could not be heard anymore. We knew the water had swallowed her the moment her voice was lost. That is a classic example of high ethics. She was devoted to her work. Her job was informing others of the disaster befalling them. She put others' lives before hers. She died but she had saved many other lives.

"As medical workers, we cannot reject patients merely because they have a contagious disease or the like. My patients are always my priority. I treated my SARS and COVID-19 patients just like I did my other patients."

"Many thanks indeed, Dr. Liu!"